Dancing with the Dead

Dancing with the Dead

For information, address:

BearManor Media
P. O. Box 71426
Albany, GA 31708

bearmanormedia.com

Typesetting and layout by John Teehan

Published in the USA by BearManor Media

ISBN—978-1-59393-994-6

Dancing with the Dead

by
Jameson Parker

BearManor Media

2017

For Steve and Beverly

For Dan and Sonja

And for Rowland

Calm and constant harbors in my stormy life

Dancing with the Dead

THEY COME FOR HER ALMOST EVERY NIGHT. *Their faces are jumbled and mismatched, so that honest gauchos she knew and worked with for fifty years wear the filthy rags of the homeless or the green uniforms of the military, and sometimes the faces morph before her from the known and loved to the brutal and evil and feared, so that none can be trusted, not even the known. In these dreams she is young again and has a beautiful young woman's primal fear of the roving gangs that surround her, laughing with anticipation, touching her with the barrels of their machine guns, reaching for her as she pants in terror. Sometimes a giant black man with matted dreadlocks and a filthy trench coat fights his way through to her, swinging his broom over his head, driving the child soldiers away, and she clings to him, inhaling the sour acrid smell of his unwashed body as once she inhaled the smoke from the censer, knowing it is the odor of Christ and love and peace, things she has not felt for many years. Other nights the black man is not there and she wakes calling his name or the name of her dead husband. Sometimes she is in the bushes of Griffith Park and the soldiers are dressed as the homeless, only their machine guns giving them away. Sometimes she is in the pastures and marshes of home and the soldiers rise up from behind tufts of pampas grass, behind fire ant mounds,*

1

behind the still shapes of the cattle, even from behind the nervous, grazing horses. Other times she stands in the darkened library where once they sat with their drinks, her hand braced against the tall cases, the dusty, comforting smell of books in her nostrils, looking again out the window at the lights of the trucks as they approach down the long allée of linden trees from the hardtop, her heart in her throat, choking her, knowing there will never be enough time, she will never get away, knowing she will be disappeared.

"¡Dése prisa, Señora! ¡Por Dios!"

And she turns to hurry, to run, but never to escape.

Part I

Argentina, Entre Rios Province, 1910

SHE WAS BORN IN A HOUSE on the bluffs of the Paraná River. The house was large and white and built to capture any breeze that might drift across the floodplain from the unpredictable and sometimes treacherous river. The town of Paraná—it was still little more than a village back then— was just a few kilometers away and the house was one of a dozen or so built by expatriate Englishmen to ape the stately homes of their ancestors on the banks of the Thames or Severn or Avon. Spacious English gardens surrounding Spanish-colonial houses; English habits and rituals with Spanish-speaking servants; English business practicality and industry with Spanish siestas in the tropical heat; English tea and *café con leche* struggling for supremacy on the banks of a river named in the tongue of an Indian tribe once famed and feared for its ferocity and cannibalism. That was the English enclave in Paraná at the beginning of the 20th century.

The doctor who delivered her, José Barragán, maintained a British Victorian decorum intended to reassure his English patrons, some of whom he had delivered himself over half a century earlier. They had been born here, some of their parents had been born here, even a few of their grandparents had been born here, but they considered

3

themselves Englishmen before they considered themselves Argentineans.

Dr. Barragán was seventy-eight. He was not the only doctor in Paraná, but he was the only one on a basis of almost equal standing with his English patients. He had traveled enough and seen enough of England to know that even if he had British blood and a British name, a mere doctor would be unlikely to be considered the equal of families whose names were in Burke's and Debrett's, and it didn't bother him. His own family had been Spanish royalists and he had grown up with the decayed elegance and sad pride of a family that backed the wrong side. But his education, and particularly his medical training in Germany, had made him sensitive to the needs and beliefs of his wealthy European patrons. He had seen with his own eyes a native Guaraní girl give birth in the dirt to a boy who lived to be eighteen and might have lived to be eighty-one if he hadn't been shot, so he had his own theories about sanitation, but he maintained a scrupulous degree of cleanliness to go with the decorum and high stiff collars and three-piece suits. Cleanliness, elegance, a European urbanity, and fluency in four languages, those were the things that made him popular and trusted.

Her father waited downstairs on the veranda overlooking a rigidly meticulous rose garden, oyster shell paths as straight as Roman roads, intersected by others at crisp right angles, Euclidean formality imposed on a voluptuous riot of scent and color. This wasn't his first waltz—a boy had been born dead and a daughter had died at six months—but his wife's screams were beginning to rattle his nerves and he wished to brace himself for any eventuality.

For John Fanshawe those screams were symbolic of the differences between England and Argentina. In England he would never have heard them. The sheer size of his ancestral home would have ensured that. Hovering around that thought like an astigmatic halo of the thought itself, was the awareness that his not hearing screams wouldn't in any way diminish his wife's pain, but in his own anxiety and distress he was willing to grasp at any idea that offered the illusion of comfort: women were designed and intended for child bearing, so surely they wouldn't—shouldn't—experience that much pain, not as much as was indicated by those dreadful sounds upstairs.

And then suddenly, silence. The stopping of screams was so abrupt that other, unnoticed sounds became magnified, the droning of bees, the squabbling of parakeets at the end of the garden, the distant barking of a dog somewhere toward the town. He moved around to the side of the house directly below his wife's bedroom, but there was still nothing, no screams, no voices, no baby crying, no weeping of servants, a silence more nerve-racking than the cries of pain. He went back to the veranda and through the double doors into the cool dark of the entry and stood at the foot of the stairs. After a time, five minutes, perhaps ten, a door closed upstairs and he heard footsteps. Dr. Barragán appeared, peering over the railing of the gallery as he walked to the head of the stairs, jacket off, shirtsleeves rolled up, waistcoat and gold watch chain still in place.

"Mr. Fanshawe, please." He opened his arms, palms up. "Come. You have a daughter who waits for you. Your wife too, she waits."

John Fanshawe started up the stairs. "Is she healthy? Is she well?"

"Which? Ah," the doctor shrugged elaborately. "It does not matter which. Both are well and healthy. But," he took one step down and put his hand out to urge the other on with a waving of his fingers, "I think it might be a good thing if there were no more babies. Mrs. Fanshawe is not built for having babies so easily as some others. It might be a good thing to stop now." He put his hand on the new father's shoulder. "Yes?"

"I shall consult with Mrs. Fanshawe, when she is feeling up to the task." As stiff and formal as his own rose garden, but he tempered it with, "Of course we shall take your advice into consideration." After all, Dr. Barragán might be Spanish—more or less; there had been so much lamentable interbreeding in Argentina over the past three hundred years—but he was a respected institution in Paraná, his hackney and shay trotting through all parts of the town at all hours and in all weathers.

She was christened Pamela, after her paternal grandmother, and whether he consulted with his wife, or whether for other reasons, she was an only child, a circumstance that would have unforeseeable consequences seventy-two years later. Her father didn't hold her on that first day, but contented himself with gazing down at the tiny, red-faced bundle in his wife's exhausted and sweating arms.

"Well," he said, "perhaps she can play polo."

It was a joke—women didn't play polo in 1910—but it too would have unforeseen consequences. John Fanshawe was one of those Englishmen who were mad about sports: cricket, rugby, polo, tennis, golf, he played them all extremely well, and he avidly followed the successes and failures of different teams and clubs and countries, reading accounts aloud from the paper with satisfaction when his favorites triumphed, tossing the same paper aside in disgust when they lost. He was an excellent wing shot and superb horseman, the kind of man who was welcomed as a guest for a weekend of sport on Argentinean estancias or on country estates during trips back to England. He was the kind of man who expected any child of his to be an effortlessly gifted athlete bristling with self-confidence, and in Pamela he got just that.

In the barns and manicured pastures behind the house he kept teams of hackneys for his various carriages, thoroughbreds for pleasure, and tough, bucket-headed little polo ponies for the sport that had been brought to Argentina only thirty years earlier, and it was here, surrounded by horses and semi-domesticated *mestizo* gauchos, that Pamela grew up. In the house facing the distant river she absorbed the ruling-class mentality of English parents who could trace their roots back to bloody successes at Crécy on one side and to a Machiavellian ancestor who was made an earl by Henry IV himself on the other. In the barns, amid the horses and polo ponies, she absorbed the mythology and freedom of hard-riding, hard-fighting, hard-loving gauchos.

At the beginning of the twentieth century Argentina and America shared a common mythology of wide-open spaces, free-range cattle and untamed gauchos or cowboys. In both countries the myth was greater than the reality had ever been, and the gauchos and cowboys were vanishing, but myth always lends more coherence and continuity to a country than any degree of reality. The gauchos had a national identity long before there was any nation. Wherever and whenever possible they clung to their old life by working on ranches. When that wasn't possible, they worked for wealthy Englishmen who kept horses, so Pamela Fanshawe grew up playing furious games on horseback, sucking *yerba maté* through silver *bombillas*, and listening to the boastful songs and stories of hard-bitten, sunburned male nannies with long knives, fast and frequently bloody, called a *facón* and carried behind the back, thrust into a broad cloth waistband. She was so completely bilingual that as a small child she was sometimes uncertain which language she was speaking and once, when she was four, ran up to her mother in the formal rose garden to ask how to say *caballo* in Spanish, an incident that became part of family lore. A wild, long-legged, long-haired, fair-skinned girl who could swing a polo mallet or throw *boleadoras* with equal ease. What she couldn't or wouldn't do was wear a dress with any degree of grace, and at thirteen her parents shipped her off to the Whitfield Old Hall School in Surrey.

The Edwardian era had ended with the beginning—or end, depending on your point of view—of the Great War, but no one had broken the news to the headmistress of Whitfield Old Hall. In fact, some of her students doubted she even knew the old queen had died, and she clung to modes of dress and behavior as outdated in their own way as Dr. Barragán's. For Pamela it was a time of cold and damp of body and soul. Instead of horses there were translations of Horace, piano lessons in place of polo ponies. The rough male companionship of her father's stable was replaced with icy cliques determined by class (of both kinds) and the social sadism peculiar to children.

"Argentina?! My God. It's not even a bloody colony. *Nobody* goes to Argentina. Isn't it somewhere frightfully barbaric, like South America or someplace awful?"

And Pamela longed to do frightfully barbaric things with a gaucho's *facón*.

She was saved by her skill at games and absolute fearlessness and by a gift for dance.

New and outrageous, even shocking, dances were sashaying through the post-war world. All across Europe girls with short hair and shorter dresses, cloche hats and flat chests, were scandalizing their parents' generation with moves and steps that proved the end was near and the world was sinking to perdition in a hand basket. The headmistress determined Whitfield Old Hall would be a rock of propriety standing firm against the incoming tide of degradation and turpitude, and the natural result was that whenever the common room door could be closed, the girls pulled up the waistbands of their dresses to raise their hemlines and did things that would have stopped the old lady's heart.

The daughter of the American Ambassador introduced the black bottom and the Charleston. The Honorable Lady Portsmouth-Boles, whose parents lived in Mayfair, introduced the rumba and the foxtrot. And Pamela Fanshawe immortalized herself by introducing the Rio de la Plata tango.

Behind the closed and guarded door the girls slid across the floor, graceful as young jaguars, twined in each other's arms, lids lowered in earnest parody of Rudolph Valentino's myopic squint that was erroneously interpreted as passion, murmuring words written at the bottom of the world's screens—Miss Fanshawe, my darling! Let me take you in my arms and kiss you!—one, two, three, four, turn, two, three four, the girls on the floor pulling down their dresses and the girl at the piano shifting instantly into a waltz whenever a knock on the door warned of an approaching adult.

For four years she lived in England, her father timing his business trips with her holidays. He and her mother would sail back and forth on the *Mauretania*, or the vener-

able *Olympic*, known as Old Reliable, only recently convert-
ed from coal to oil, and refitted to reflect up-to-the-minute
luxury.

The family stayed at the Connaught in London and
used it as a base for their travels, her father's business schedule permitting. Once they went to France which, for John
and Charlotte Fanshawe, meant Paris exclusively. Oh, yes,
there were other parts of the country, but they weren't inter-
ested in any of that, and besides, the rural French were so,
well, French. Once they went to Lincolnshire to show their
daughter the ruins of what had been Charlotte Fanshawe's
family's ancestral estate, a bleak and forbidding tower
perched on a man-made mound between fen and field,
where an unknown distant ancestor ("It happened back
in the 1400's, darling, so I'm not really terribly clear as to
the precise connection. A grandmother with ten or eleven
greats attached, I believe.") threw herself off the battlements
rather than be taken alive by the men besieging the walls.
("She probably had a pretty good idea of what would happen to her if they got her.")

Her mother explained the ruined tower had been built
using the stones of an earlier ruin, and that earlier tower
had in turn been built on Roman foundations, but that the
mound itself predated all of that, so Pamela was left with a
sense of history in horizontal layers, of the past sinking further and further into the earth, pressed down by succeeding
generations, awaiting another layer.

And one year they went to her father's ancestral manse
in Lancashire where history presented itself laterally. The
place was a hodge-podge of architectural styles, succes-
sive generations adding onto it over the centuries as they
wished without any attempt to rectify the whole into a co-

herent entity, until a fragmented history of England from the Norman invasion to Queen Anne could be traced in its multiple façades. It had been left, along with the title, the lands, and all the money, to John Fanshawe's older brother, one of the Old Contemptibles—"the gallant Old Contemptibles"—who marched off to fight the Hun, perhaps in place of his own son, who was born with a series of emotional and physical anomalies, including a twisted spine and a club foot. The older brother distinguished himself by being one of the very first officers ever to die of gas, chlorine gas. The son, limping and listing, only a few years younger than his uncle, distinguished himself by refusing to receive them and they stayed at a local inn with damp sheets, bad food and excellent beer.

"We never got along, my brother and I." They were seated in the inn's pub, pushing beef the color of ashes around on their plates. John Fanshawe seemed curiously unruffled by their cold lack of reception. "He made it very clear I'd be thrown out on my own as soon as the Pater died. Threw Mother out, too. Fortunately, I was doing well enough by then I could buy a flat for her. I offered to bring her to Paraná, but she wouldn't hear of leaving England. She came down with food poisoning as a girl, traveling in Italy, and vowed never to leave England again. Couldn't understand why I left."

Pamela looked at the tasteless, texture-less meat in front of her and remembered the slabs, whole haunches, the gauchos cooked on iron frames angled over coals spitting and smoking as the fat dripped onto them, and how, with only salt and wood smoke as seasoning, it was better than any food she had had in England, even at the Connaught. They sat, wrapped in wool, huddled by the fire, colder on a summer evening in northern England than any winter night at home. Perhaps, she thought, I'll imitate that unknown eponymous grandmother and never leave Argentina again.

Los Angeles, 1982

SHIT. LOOK AT ALL THIS. Trash everywhere. I fill that trash can there clear up to the top in four days, three sometimes, and damn trash truck don't come but once a week and not even then sometimes. Make you wonder. All that trash just right here on this one corner. One corner out of thousands and thousands of corners all across this city, and this ain't but one city out of thousands all across this country. Think about that, Lieutenant. Think about how much trash that is. I can't even conceive how much that is, how much space it take to hold all that trash. The kind of thing you think about it too much, it make you start howling and moaning again. Not that anybody give a damn anymore. Maybe that's why that trash truck don't always come like it supposed to. Maybe it just get overwhelmed, so much trash they ain't enough trucks to pick it all up. Course, this the only corner I sweep, and they ain't trash cans on every corner, but trash is everywhere. And most of it paper. Some of it's walking and talking, but most of it's newspaper. It's like they make them newspapers just so people got something to throw down on the street.

That's how I first learned how to read. Mama had gone, so Mamaw used to read to us all the time, me and my brother, read to us out of the papers, out of the magazines they was

13

throwing away from that house she cleaned. Mrs. Stone. See that? Thirty years ago, more, but I remember. Ain't nothing wrong with my memory, Lieutenant. Mrs. Stone. Big old gal. Leastways she was to me back then. Probably wasn't no bigger than a catbird, but when you just a kid, everything and everybody look bigger than what they are. Especially white people. Back then, white people was the biggest people they was. Boy, don't you be touching that. Boy, take this out to the garbage, less'n you want to keep it. Boy, ain't no colored allowed in here. That's how all them white people kept themselves so big. But that house my Mamaw cleaned, that was big. Big! I remember back then we lived out on other side of town, past the depot and all, me and Mamaw and Bill. That was my brother, Bill. *Oh, Bill, I love you so and I always will.* And we lived in that house out there, three of us, but you could of took our whole house, the whole damn thing, picked it up and put it just in the kitchen of Mrs. Stone's house, kitchen, pantry, laundry room, like that. That's how big that house was my Mamaw cleaned.

But all them papers and magazines Mrs. Stone threw out, *The Delta Democrat*, *Life*, *Saturday Evening Post*, *Good Housekeeping*, my Mamaw would carry them all home and read them to us. Education was real important to her 'cause she never had none. Taught her own self to read. Her daddy was a sharecropper, been born a slave, and she grew up out there on one of them plantations somewhere, used to tell us all about how the old white boy owned the place would trot by in a shiny buggy all dressed up in a white suit with a white straw hat and them two horses stepping to reach the sun, and she said it was like looking at the Almighty His own self driving by. The Almighty. He white, you know, Lieutenant. White like you. Black people praying to Him all over the whole damn world, but He's a white man in a white suit driving a team of high-stepping horses. Even in church every Sunday morning, black church, with everybody singing and praying, we was singing and praying to a white man. Shit.

But back then when my Mamaw was little they didn't have no schools for no sharecroppers' daughters. Didn't have them, didn't want them. If you can't read or write, then maybe you never figure there's any better life than picking cotton year in, year out. Mamaw had to teach herself all by herself after she was grownup. So she didn't want none of her blood not having no education, and between her and school, me and Bill learned our letters and all better than most of the white kids at their school. And not just reading and writing and 'rithmatic. See, all them papers and magazines and all was written by white people, for white people, about white people. There wasn't no black folks anywhere in any of them. There wasn't no black folks in the whole wide world for all you could tell from reading them magazines. Black folks didn't exist in the white world. Just white people everywhere. So me and Bill, we learned how to talk white. We read all them magazines, and he take me down to listen to the white people in front of the big houses and passing in and out of the courthouse and all like that, and then we go on home and imitate them when Mamaw wasn't around. Ha! By the time I went into the Army, shit, I could talk white better then any of them non-coms. "Lieutenant, we have aerial surveillance showing enemy movement in the following sectors." Ha! Shit. Course, you didn't talk like that around no white people. Mississippi back then, talking that way could get you strung up in the town square, and in the Army, shit, you stay a buck private the rest of your natural life.

Would have been better off, maybe, huh? Both of us.

No. I ain't going to go there. I ain't going to let myself go there. I talk to Jesus everyday, ask him to help me keep out of there, talk to Him, talk to you, talk to Bill too, Mamaw sometimes, trying to stay out of that place, and I'm doing good, sweep my corner here, no drugs or nothing, and stay away from that bad place. Just sweep and talk to you, talk to Jesus. Keep sweeping, make things clean again.

You think it strange, me talking to Bill and Mamaw? Why's that, Lieutenant? Ain't no different from talking to Jesus. Only difference, He been dead going on two thousand years and Bill and Mamaw only been dead maybe fifteen. Millions of people all over the whole damn world, they talk to Jesus every day and ain't nobody think they crazy. But you talk to your loved ones only been dead a few years, people think you ought to be locked up somewhere. Don't make no sense to me.

Look at all this, Lieutenant. Trash everywhere. Perfectly good trash can right there. All they got to do is walk another twenty feet, but no, they drop it right where they standing. Wasn't no trash around my Mamaw's house. Shit. Wasn't no trash around any black folks' house. Back then black folks wasn't rich enough to have trash. But now, something's changed, something's different. I don't understand it. It's been a long time and things has changed, but I don't like it, so I just keep cleaning it up. Can't change the whole world, can't even change the whole damn city, but I can sweep this corner up, keep everything spic and span.

Argentina, Entre Rios Province, 1937

"**YOUR FATHER LOVED** this ridiculous house. I think your mother saw more clearly what an inappropriate disaster it was—she asked me once what on earth my grandfather was thinking when he built it—but your father loved it. He shot pheasant and stag and wild boar at its counterpoint, its inspiration, in Bohemia—Czechoslovakia now. That would have been around 1895 or so, a few years before he came out here, after his brother inherited everything and threw him out."

They sat in the library, the late afternoon light slanting in through the leaves of the linden trees, the parakeets outside calling raucous and harsh in endless territorial dispute.

"The great thing, Pamela, about the old British belief in primogeniture, is that it helps propagate empire building. If you're an ambitious younger son, running the family estates isn't an option. Even if you're not ambitious, if you're a feckless fool, it isn't an option. But if you're ambitious, cut off without money or resources, or with just a small stipend, the world beckons. Argentina, America, Africa, India, Ceylon. Look at what younger sons have done for England. Look at what your father achieved. He was no scientist. He was no engineer. But he was smart enough to understand the economic possibilities of refrigeration. Look at what my grandfather achieved here at *El Rincón*." He waved his glass around the room to indicate the ridiculous imitation of a central European shooting lodge and the surrounding land. "The sun never sets on the British Empire, and it never will."

"I don't believe America is part of the British Empire anymore, and Argentina never was."

She tried to infuse it with more dry and pointed humor than she felt. She knew what her husband was doing and was grateful to him. He loved to wax philosophical, to pontificate, emphasizing his age, his education, his masculine understanding of the sweep of history and world events with just enough pomposity to inspire her to deflate him. It was one of their rituals, one of the comfortable patterns of shared private humor that develop in married life, performance and response twined together before the private footlights of marriage, a graceful and mutually enjoyed ritual exchange that reinforced bonds and emotions and vows. He would blow his beautiful, intelligent, articulate bubble larger and larger until, unable to resist any longer, she would prick it, and after his rueful and bemused look they would share a laugh, a smile, a moment of intimacy as uniquely their own as their knowledge of each other's bodies. And now, their first day home after burying her parents, he was trying to bring her emotions back to normalcy.

"But America was once, and even after their upstart rebellion younger sons helped shape and develop the land. Many of their great ranches and businesses were started by Englishmen, just as they were here. Of course, America isn't part of the British Empire anymore, more is the pity, and Argentina never was, but the principle is the same. Argentina is dependent on England. General Justo can strut and imitate Mussolini or that pompous little idiot in Germany, he can rant to his heart's content and make as much meaningless noise as those parakeets, but he doesn't dare upset his own apple cart. He can persecute the Radicals, he can talk all he wants about socioeconomic control and a strong central government and all the rest of his nonsense, but he will leave us alone. He will leave all the British families alone. The beef we raise brings in too much money for him to risk annoying the Crown or Prime Minister Baldwin. We will be safe."

She believed him. She confused the rhythms of their life with the rhythms of the world's slow turning, so that late afternoons in the library, the moving of cattle that could have been left to the gauchos were it not so enjoyable, the wild polo games on their and other ranches from Buenos Aires to Cordoba, the dinners with cultured and educated Englishmen and Spaniards and Italians and Germans, Argentineans all, the shooting parties in the brush with fine shotguns by Purdey and Holland & Holland and Merkel, and the clouds of dove that darkened the sky, that world, that life, would last forever. She and Ian would sit in this soft late afternoon light till the end of their days, in this library with its fourteen-foot ceilings, in this ugly and architecturally inappropriate re-creation of a central European shooting lodge whose only real virtue was a square central tower that sucked the leaden heat of the day up like a chimney, on their 18,000 hectares where cattle and horses grazed, a continuation of their world stretching into the future and unaffected by dancing madmen in Germany or ranting, heavy-jawed Italians in black shirts or the unending chaos that seemed to envelop the world, and someday, way in the future, their places would be taken by yet unborn children and grandchildren.

"It was men like your father who brought this country into the twentieth century. My father simply kept on with what his father had started, a tradition of animal husbandry that has been around since the days of the Pharaohs, but refrigeration…! There are two kinds of genius, Pamela. There are men who invent things, and there are men who see the usefulness of things other men have invented. Your father was the second kind of genius, but he was unquestionably a genius. It's why I married you."

She smiled at him automatically, a conditioned response to a familiar gambit. Sexual banter was another ritual, a private shorthand for expressing sentiments he rarely verbalized. It might begin with any one of a number of permutations. If she wore a dress he found particularly attractive or provocative he might say, "I only married you for your body." If she delighted him with some witty comment or erudite observation, it became, "I only married you for your brain." If she scored a goal or made an exceptional play in one of their endless polo matches, then it would be, "I only married you to get you on my team." Whatever the variation, the gambit was one he used frequently as a prelude to taking her by the hand and leading her upstairs, the key turned in the lock, clothes dropped where they stood, laughter and cries smothered in the pillows. "I only married you for…" was always accompanied by a suggestive raising of a single eyebrow, a movement so linked to that sentence and its sequel that at dinner parties, at receptions in the British embassy in Buenos Aires, at polo matches as they stood surrounded by other players and horses and grooms, anywhere, he had only to twitch the corner of that left eyebrow to make a connection, sometimes to reduce her to prurient blushes and helpless giggles.

But not this time. It was still far too hot, they had only just finished dressing for dinner, and they both knew Lorenzo would come in to announce the food was on the table in just a few more minutes. So now she smiled at her husband and understood in a little flash of clairvoyance that this particular ritual banter was intended to be anodyne, for him as much as for her, and with that realization came the understanding of what he too must be feeling. Ian was only nine years younger than her father and they had been close friends and business associates for almost twenty years. Her father had bought the beef Ian's father, and then Ian, raised, shipping it to England in the refrigerated containers her father had helped design. She had grown up watching her husband play polo with her father, play tennis with her father, shoot with her father, discuss business with her father, attend weddings and funerals and christenings with her father, out-maneuver one chaotic and grasping regime after another with her father, and yet ever since they got the news he had never shown any emotion beyond sympathy and concern for her. For a week, since the ringing of the phone—that dreadful middle-of-the-night sound, like waking to the kicking in of a door or smashing of a window or the scream of a loved one; a heart-racing, nauseating sound in the dark—he had been, as always, the tower of strength, the practical manager of details, dealing with the provincial police, having the wrecked and mangled Packard hauled away, arranging travel, notifying friends, a cousin back in Glastonbury in Somerset, calling the bishop in Paraná, selecting coffins and headstones, busying himself in a thousand helpful and thoughtful ways as she lay paralyzed with grief, but he had never wept or raged or lost even an iota of control. And now, "It's why I married you." She wanted to hug him.

Instead, she played a variation of the game: "You married me because you couldn't help yourself. You couldn't resist me."

He smiled back at her.

"Quite true. I watched you grow up for ten years and never thought of you as anything other than an exceptionally nice and pretty little girl and then one day not long after you came home from England I went to your house to discuss something with your father... what was it?... export tariffs or something dreadful like that, and you were in the front hall, near the clock, and you bent down to pat that shaggy dog you had then, the giant dust mop, what was his name?"

"Merlin."

"Merlin. You bent over to pat him and I could see right down the front of your dress. I could see your breasts."

"You dreadful old pervert."

"Yes. I saw your breasts, the most beautiful and perfect breasts I had ever seen, and I couldn't breathe. Quite literally, my dear. You took my breath away, I wanted you so. And with that thought—if you can call that a thought—came the realization I had been in love with you for a long time. Probably ever since I first met you when you were seven or eight or whatever."

"Love or lust?"

She was mocking him, and only a week ago he would have followed her lead, playing up the lustful cradle robber, making reference to things and people and events she had no knowledge of, all the lacunae of a twenty-three year age difference. She had never heard of Marie Lloyd and barely knew who Harry Lauder was. The battles of the war (for he still held British citizenship and had fought for England) were nothing more than place names to her, Ypres, Verdun,

Somme; the songs of the war he whistled, *The Bells of Hell*, and *Oh, It's A Lovely War!*, were unknown to her. Even where it involved a subject near and dear to her heart the age difference left holes: she had no idea that Cyllene, the grand old stud of Ojo de Agua, grandsire of many of their own horses, had once been the greatest race horse of his day in England, winning the 1899 Ascot Gold Cup carrying one hundred and forty pounds. Ian had been at school in England at the time and had been taken to see the race, eleven years before she was even born. These generational gaps—more than a single generation—were things he and her father had both teased her about whenever they got together, playing two wise old men to her naïve child. But now he said simply, "Love. At seven, at seventeen, and now at twenty-seven. Someday at seventy-seven. Of course, I'll be 100 then and may not be too certain who you are."

She moved to him and stood beside him, but instead of looking up at her, he put his drink down and placed his hand on her hip and canted his head, resting it just above her pubic bone. He said nothing, but he sighed deeply, as if this contact, this touching her with hand and head, were something he had waited for a long time, perhaps as if that were as close as he could ever come to expressing his own grief. Or perhaps simply as if he were very tired. God knows he had the right.

She didn't care what his reasons were. Such moments of intimacy brought her more peace and comfort than anything else and were always associated with this room. It reminded her of sitting on the sofa with her mother on the porch of their house in Paraná, trying to catch whatever breeze might come up from the river, talking or reading, and her mother's hand would rise up slowly, absently, often without even looking, almost like something independent of its owner's volition, and rest lightly on the back of Pamela's neck, gently playing with the wisps of hair at her nape, stroking, tickling gently, her fingers always cool, so cool and refreshing, no matter how brutal the heat, making a contact that was free of any demand or desire, simply the mother's hand touching the neck of a body that had once been part of her. That kind of intimacy.

She began to cry. Not to sob—there was no sound or convulsing of her body—but tears began to come out of her eyes as if memory had opened a valve in her body. She put her own hands on the back of her husband's head—a tear splashed on the back of one hand—the sleek, carefully groomed head she knew so well and loved so much, so perfectly and evenly streaked with gray that it was almost the color of a gun barrel with much of the bluing worn away. Someday he too would go, leaving her behind to try and disentangle the memories and emotions of their shared life, and when he did, these were the moments she would cherish, mount carefully in the scrapbook of her heart, her husband's hand on her hip, his head resting just above her pubic bone, in the immutable tranquility of this dusty library.

The door opened and Lorenzo appeared, stopping abruptly at the sight of them. Ian raised his head.

"It's alright, Lorenzo," he said in Spanish. "We're both a little tired. That's all. Is dinner ready?"

"On the table, Señor."

"We are on our way."

Lorenzo withdrew, and Pamela turned, but instead of standing Ian looked up at his young wife, his hand still on her hip, hers on his shoulder, and for a moment they stayed like that, looking at each other, content in each other's presence, in their shared loss, their shared sorrow.

Los Angeles, 1982

MAMAW KNEW ABOUT SCHOOLS some way even when she was little. See, the way it work back then, when you sharecropping, you raising cotton for the white man. All of it, every bit, every last damn boll, it all belong to him. On his part, he give you a cabin, huh, not much more than that cardboard box I been sleeping in, a little patch of dirt around it to raise your okra and peas and such, and that's about the end of it. You want flour? You buy it from his store. You want a pair overalls? You buy them from his store. You want shoes, salt, corn syrup, grits? Buy them from the white man's store. Only, if you ain't got no money, you buy them on credit, then what you owe is deducted from whatever he supposed to give you for the cotton you picked all during the year. Only you can't never pick enough cotton to make up the difference of what you owe, never mind any getting ahead. Work like a mule, start picking when it still dark, don't quit till it get dark again, but it don't make no never mind. You ain't never going to get ahead. White man reads the scale when he weighs your cotton. White man reads how much you owe out of a book he keeps. White man figures out the difference. You don't never get to see the books and the scale and the writing, and even if you did, it wouldn't mean nothing in this world 'cause if you colored, back in that time and that place, you can't read. White man don't want you to read, cause if you can read, you might start figuring out just exactly why you wasn't never going to pick enough cotton to get ahead.

So out there in the country there wasn't no schools for no colored. Not back then. Mamaw was smart enough she figured it out, figured out cleaning houses was a whole lot better than peeling the hide off your fingers picking cotton bolls. Fingers bleeding, dragging a bag, sun beating down, snakes and deer flies, sweat rolling off you, never holding a dollar in your hand from one year to the next. Cleaning houses was a damn picnic to her. She made it into town walking all that way when she was still just a little girl, went to work cleaning, never left that town again. Spent the whole rest of her life right there, walking back and forth, up that little no-name possum-trot where we lived to Catalpa Street, along Catalpa past the old gin mill—it was still running when me and Bill was real young, but after the fire they built the new one a little farther out towards the highway—short left on Rifle Ferry, past the depot, then right on Forrest and past the shops and the courthouse and the businesses all the way to them big old houses like something you dream, wedding cakes shaded by trees that was old when the first white men came bringing their black slaves with them, their niggers, to clear the land and kill the Indians and dig the clay to make the bricks, cut the trees to make the beams and columns and verandas they would clean but never sit on. I could still walk it. Nothing wrong with my memory.

No more than a girl when she did it, walking first along the highway that was just an old dirt road back then, ribbon of dust or ribbon of mud, hiding in the woods or in the ditch every time she saw or heard a wagon or a man on horse or mule or on foot, black or white, spending the night huddled up against the base of a big old hickory tree and not sleeping a wink the whole night through she was so scared, and then walking on, to the town where she had an aunt she had never seen but only heard of, an aunt who might not be alive or even real. And she just a little girl, ten or twelve or maybe some other number of years old, she wasn't sure.

I was almost a grown man when she told me all that and I tell you what, Lieutenant, I never took no trip in my whole entire life, not to Fort Benning, Viet Nam, Japan, LA, no place, no matter how far away, nothing was ever as far as that twenty miles into town must have been to that little girl. Saw her first car in town, said it scared her more than spending the night alone in the woods. She knew what it was, she'd heard of them, but she'd never seen one and it scared her. Think about that, LT. I didn't know much when I went to Fort Benning, but I never saw nothing so new it scared me the way that car scared her. No machine or gun or grenade launcher or tank or nothing was as new to me as that car was to her. Nothing the white man or the Viet Cong could do to me was as scary or as foreign as that twenty miles or that car was to my Mamaw.

But what you going to do when you just ten or twelve years old, you don't even know how old you are, but you know there's got to be something better than a life of bleeding fingers and burning sun and never having nothing? What you going to do? Sixteen years old I knew there was something better out there, and I knew or thought or believed the Army was the way to get it, but that was fifty years or more after she walked those twenty miles that separated two whole different ways of living, different ways of being. The only two ways there was for colored folks back then.

The aunt was real and alive. I don't even know her name, but she got my Mamaw work in one of them big houses, ten or maybe twelve or maybe some other number of years when she started walking that walk through the town that she did for over fifty years. Different houses, different white folks. Sometimes two or three generations in one house, or two or three different owners of one house, and Mamaw passed from one owner to the next like the slave days was still there, like a piece of something that belonged to the house that wasn't quite part of the house, the way a family might leave one of them wrought iron benches in yard for the next family, an old fountain or a birdbath maybe. More than fifty years she walked that walk and she only worked in three different houses and one of them burned down or it would of just been two.

She been walking from one side of that town to the other for ten years or more before she got married. Shad. Shadrach, from the Bible, you know. Big as a house. She told us, me and Bill, when he walked in the door of that shack he took her to on the possum trot with no name, when he walked in that door he blocked out all the sun and the light like a door his own self he was so big. She didn't have no picture of him, just his name in the Bible where she wrote it down after she learned her letters, so I never got to see him, but I reckon I take after him some, size and all.

He worked up there in the gin and he watched her walking by in the mornings and back in the evenings. Watched her grow up walking back and forth. And she seen him watching, but he never spoke no word to her, not one, not once, until the day when she was maybe fifteen or sixteen or seventeen, not a girl no more, but not yet a woman neither, and he step down off the little porch in front of the gin and walk out to the path where she was passing by.

Mamaw say, "It wasn't like having no man step in front of you. It was like having a team of mules pull a cotton wagon in your way. He block the whole street, he so big, like he was a piece of history itself changing everything with its movement. He looked down at me and said, 'Girl, when the time is right, when you ready, I'm going to marry you.' Just like that. And then he turn and walk back to the gin and keep right on working, and I kept on walking through the town, but my heart was going so and I couldn't tell if it was excitement or love or fear or what it might be. I just know my heart was pushing my ribs right out through my dress."

But more years went by before the time was right. She never told me who made that decision. Knowing Mamaw, it had to be her. A dozen Shads wouldn't of been big enough or strong enough to make that woman change whatever path she chose by even an inch. People talk about Southern ladies and how strong they will is, all soft and buttery like a biscuit on the outside, but tempered, polished, honed steel on the inside. Well, Mamaw was a Southerner, and she was a lady. She was maybe black or colored or negro or nigger, depending on who was doing the talking and the judging, but even the trashiest rednecks could see what she was.

When they married he took her to that house on the possum trot where me and Bill was raised and our Mama before us. Mama was the onliest child Mamaw and Shad had before he got hisself killed.

Most towns got something, some big event that marks them for all the rest of they history, so when you talking and trying to let folks know when something or other happened you say, That was before the flood of such and such, or That was the year after the fire of such and such, just like you might say something happened out here before or after the big earthquake in San Francisco. It don't even matter if you know exactly what year it happen in 'cause all you doing is setting a time in your mind. In our town it was called the Big Derailment.

Shad was maybe taking a wagon load of bales to get picked up at the depot, or he was maybe down there to pick something up for the gin, I don't know for sure, but he was there with a wagon and a team of mules, waiting. Not every train stopped in that little town, and I guess he was sitting up there on the wagon, or maybe standing by the mules or talking to somebody, when an express came through heading down to Jackson or up to Memphis and some damn fool threw the switch at the wrong time and that train took out just about everything for about a quarter of a mile.

Mamaw saved the paper that wrote up the account and that's one of the first things I can remember reading all by myself. I wasn't allowed to touch it, all yellow and crumbling away and all, but I remember sitting at the table where she put it out more careful than she did even with the Bible, and working out those words about the destruction it caused, and how four men, including the engineer, was killed, and two mules, and seven negroes.

I was, oh, I don't know, seven, eight, maybe nine when I read that old paper, but you know, LT, I was a grown man and in the Army over there in Viet Nam and everything before I ever thought about the significance of how that was written up. Four men, two mules, and seven negroes. In that order. That's how it was back in them days, shit, even when I was growing up it was still pretty much like that. In that time when my granddaddy was killed, a good mule might cost you $25, but a negro didn't cost you nothing at all. Wasn't even counted as a man.

Argentina, Buenos Aires Province, 1952

LATER SHE ALWAYS ASSOCIATED DEATH and the ombú tree.

There were neatly planted trees everywhere at La Perdida. Queen palms lined the drive in and jacarandas framed both sides of the field, but the single ombú was ancient, monstrous, prehistoric. It might have shaded Sebastian Cabot. It might have shaded Adam and Eve. It shaded the players before the game, between the chukkas, and after the game as they laughed and sweated with their champagne, sitting and leaning on the enormous roots as the grooms cooled-down the ponies under the jacarandas.

She could have associated the jacarandas with death, or the queen palms, or the white side boards, or the wicker goal posts, or the distant white hacienda with its red tile roof and deep shaded verandas, but it was the ombú tree.

They drove down just past Cañuelas the afternoon before the game with some of their own horses and sixteen-year old Hipólito as a groom. La Perdida, named after a local legend about an Indian girl, was only a few kilometers outside the little town. Ernesto Pieres had bought the land and built the hacienda not for ranching or farming, but solely as a place to play polo and breed his horses. His oldest son, Eduardo was a seven-goaler who played in America

31

as a hired assassin for a multimillionaire amateur, but he returned home after his father's stroke and took over the running of La Perdida, inviting professionals and serious, well-heeled amateurs like Ian and Pamela to come drink champagne, play, try his horses, buy, put money down for stud fees, laugh under the canopy of the ombú.

The dining hall at La Perdida was only slightly smaller than the polo field. Pamela was seated next to Francisco Pieres, the youngest son, a freshly minted army lieutenant, as servants circled the table with platters of beef and bottles of pre-war Château Haut Brion. Inside the circle of wine and beef and white coats the conversation and laughter moved around the table as unselfconsciously as if the servants were deaf or made of wax.

"You've heard she has been given the title, 'The Spiritual leader of the Nation,' for God's sake?"

"Thank God she gave up this absurd idea of the vice presidency. Crowds of shirtless ones blocking the streets and chanting, '¡*Evita!* ¡*Evita!*' Such nonsense."

"That was the General Confederation of Labor, which is to say, that was Perón. What do you expect?"

"It wasn't that she gave up the idea. She's too sick. I've heard she had a hysterectomy."

"Where did you hear that?"

"Oh, I have my sources, I have friends."

"It must be true. I saw, '¡Viva el *cáncer!*' on a wall just three blocks from my home."

"Of course it's true. It's the worst kept secret in Argentina."

"You won't see it written in any newspaper."

"Not in any Argentinean paper. Perhaps *Time* Magazine."

"Then *Time* will disappear from Argentina again."

Francisco turned to Pamela.

"As an English lady, Señora Trevelyan, what do you think of the patron saint of the *descamisados*?"

"*Soy Argentino, Francisco*. I have an Argentinean passport, not an English one."

"I understand. I phrased it badly. From an English point of view, an English sensibility, what do you think of this raising of the poor on the backs of those who have made this country, the productive ones?"

"Is that what Perón is doing?"

"Of course. Why do you think I went into the army? It is safer than the universities these days. 'Shoes? Yes! Books? No!'"

"The closing of the universities is bad and counterproductive, but Eva Perón... I'm Church of England, not Catholic, but I think what she does for the poor is a wonderful expression of Christianity. It is the sort of thing Jesus urged us all to do."

"Is it? It is whispered that her foundation only puts money here," he partially pulled his wallet out of his coat, "in her own purse. They say the only purpose of that European tour was to deposit funds into a bank in Switzerland."

"I don't know about that. I don't think anyone knows the truth about that, but she gives the poor hope as well as help. She treats them with respect and love, love in the Biblical sense, and surely that is not a bad thing."

"But God himself told Moses we should respect neither the poor nor the rich, but treat both impartially."

She laughed. "Ah, Francisco, as a nominal Protestant I should know better than to debate a well-educated Catholic. Eva Perón does some good, and if she pays herself for it, well, at least more good is done than harm."

Francisco stared at her, his eyes as dark and unreadable as if he were wearing sunglasses, expressionless pools in which she imagined she could see herself reflected, strophe and antistrophe in an argument older than history. Many years later she would see him again and have a hard time reconciling the puffy lined face and white mustache with the beautiful arrogant boy who sat beside her the night before her husband's death. His eyes roamed over her face, and it was impossible to imagine what he might be thinking. At last he smiled and turned back to his dinner.

"You are very beautiful, Señora Trevelyan. Very beautiful on the outside and very beautiful on the inside."

After that they talked of other things and over Francisco's shoulder she could see her husband seated next to ancient Mrs. Pieres, Ernesto's mother, at the far end of the table. Their eyes met and when Mrs. Pieres leaned forward to slurp a spoonful of soup through ill-fitting dentures, Ian lifted his glass to Pamela and raised his left eyebrow.

The next morning Ian's color wasn't good.

"Dyspepsia, old girl, nothing more. I'll be fine after I have a cup of tea."

But he threw up after his tea and went back to their room to lie down until the game.

Francisco, the youngest and lowest-ranked player of the extended Pieres family, offered to play for the visitors if Ian wasn't well enough, but when it was time, Ian rose and put on his boots.

They assembled between the ombú and the jacarandas, the whitewashed, red tiled shed-row barn in the background, the grooms holding the saddled horses by braided rawhide head collars until time came for the bridle, the horses as sleek and gleaming as the saddles, legs wrapped in individual ranch colors to match their saddle-blankets, tails braided and tied short, some stamping and jigging, some grazing, others tied to ropes strung tightly between the jacarandas, players laying out rows of bamboo mallets by length to match their horses' height, by head shape to match their owners' preferences and needs, laying out too their leather knee guards and helmets and gloves by the folding canvas chairs under the ombú canopy, a riotous panoply of color, green and white and red and the mustard yellow jerseys of La Perdida, the soft purple of the jacaranda blossoms, the carmine of the visitors' jerseys, varying shades of leather of different ages, from new pigskin to London tan to the darkest Cuban tobacco, the variegated colors of the helmets dictated by personal preference only, laughter and voices calling, an audible hum of anticipation, an electric hum of excitement, of competition, even of youth, for all men are young again when they play polo.

There are no team loyalties in polo. The only loyalty is to the game itself, so that a player might, even between chukkas, if necessary, pull off one team's jersey and slip on another and never change or compromise his level of play. Ian and Pamela were playing for the local neighboring team and wearing carmine instead of the deep green of *El Rincón*.

Positions two and three require the greatest skill and aggression, and unless they had world-class players like Eduardo on their team, Ian always played three and Pamela two. Today, playing for the vast *Quebracho Rojo* Ranch, with the legendary father-son team of Juan and Manuel Forsythe at two and three, Pamela was at one and Ian at four.

They rode out onto the field. Ian's color was still bad and he rode holding the handle of his mallet against his stomach, but as they lined up he smiled at her and lifted his left eyebrow and for a moment—a trick of light, a trick of memory—he was the lean strong man she had married almost a quarter century ago, and she laughed as if she too were once again young enough to be moved to blushes and giggles. Then the ball was thrown.

A young man from Córdoba, only a few years older than Francisco, was playing number four for La Perdida. He was fast and aggressive and good-humored, laughing and roaring with mock outrage when Pamela rode him off the ball, grinning at her as he yelled elaborate insults in bad and obscure English. "Miserable womans from poor marshes!" The first seven-minute chukka thundered by in a blurred montage of horse's hooves, the smells of horse and leather and moist grass, the sharp crack of the ball, voices raised in excitement, the familiar thrill of the horse beneath her, separate yet part of her too, so that horse and rider became greater than the sum of their individual parts, the grace and speed and strength of the animal flowing up into her, transforming her, exalting her, the feel of the mallet in one hand, the four reins and crop in the other, sun and wind and land, timeless and immortal.

Once, near the end, she saw Ian at a gallop drop his mallet in a preliminary swing for an off-side backstroke, then hit the ball with his deadly power, driving it past her head close enough that she could hear the whirr, and as she spun her horse and drove for the goal she had a glimpse of his face, smiling with satisfaction, but that was the memory that lingered: Ian galloping away from her, slightly up in his stirrups, the broad back, the curved arc of his mallet, all four of his horse's shoes glinting at her, the blur of his mallet descending.

At the end of the chukka they trotted their horses back to the ombú. Hipólito was there to take their horses and he walked them back to the picket line as Ian and Pamela gulped water and laughed and insulted and threatened opposing team members. There wasn't time enough to sit, and Ian was leaning against one of the massive twisted roots when Hipólito reappeared with their next two ponies. Pamela reached to pick up a different mallet, and when she turned Ian was already holding his horse and preparing to mount.

"Are you feeling better?"

He looked at her over his horse's back, grinning, flushed, excited. "I feel fabulous!" He stepped up into the stirrup, but instead of swinging his leg across he pitched head-first over the horse and landed on his back at her feet.

The horse shied away, then trotted out toward the field where it dropped its head to graze, reins trailing. Someone yelled. People ran over, turned in surprise, gathered around, staring, unsure what had happened or what to do. Voices spoke in Spanish and English. "What is it?" "¿Que paso?" "What happened?" The young man from Córdoba knelt by the body and pulled off his helmet and Ian's, loosened Ian's shirt and pants and breathed down the dead man's throat, pressed rhythmically on his chest. Someone ran hard toward the house. Eduardo's wife covered her face with her hands and peered out through spread fingers. A very young child started to cry.

Pamela knelt across from the young man and put her hands under Ian's head. The hair was still as thick as it was thirty years ago when he came to the house in Paraná to talk and dine with her father and mother. She had watched the slow transition from black, the first faint streaks of grey at the temples climbing gradually up to create the gunmetal color that had leaned with fatigue and grief against her pubic bone in the library, almost completely white now, just a hint now, here and there, of the raven black, coal black, sloe black, death black hair of the only man she had known and loved. She stroked it back, wet with perspiration, so familiar, yet suddenly so foreign, so that when the young man from Córdoba finally gave up and sat back on his haunches and looked at her—a slight raising of his shoulders and eyebrows, a slight tilting of his head, a turning down of his mouth—she already knew. She had already felt something, she couldn't say what, leave the beloved body.

She scooched forward on her knees and rested his head on her lap. It seemed very important to her just then that his head not touch the ground. She had seen the recently dead before—a gaucho whose neck was snapped when his horse rolled over him; another gaucho who died in his sleep, in his bed; old Petra the housekeeper in her black dress, while walking under the lindens—but Ian's face had none of the vacuity of death. He looked very peaceful, as if he were only resting, perhaps fooling around, making a bad joke, and might at any moment rise up laughing. But that was only how he looked. The hair felt different. The perspiration was already cooling to clamminess. Something she could neither express nor even identify had left him. Something she could neither express nor even identify had left her.

Francisco knelt down on one side. Hipólito knelt down on the other. Both young men, little more than boys, put their arms around her shoulders so that their arms twined together like the roots of the ombú tree in support of her. That too would have consequences many years later.

Los Angeles, 1982

BILL, BILL. *I love you Bill and I always will.* Me and Bill, me and Bill. It was always me and Bill together. All our neighbors back there used to talk about how we always together, can't see one without the other. There was other kids around, sometimes we run around with them, play games, go swimming down in the creek, sing songs with LeRoy, run all round the town—our part of the town, I mean, the black part—but it was always me and Bill together. That's just how we was. He one year older and not as big, but Mamaw say sometimes it was more like we was twins instead of just brothers. Only thing could separate us was the United States Army.

Me and Bill, we signed up together 1964, right after the Civil Rights Act. We would of done it sooner, wanted to do it right after Medgar Evers and all the year before, but shit, Lieutenant, I wasn't but fifteen years old that year, Bill only sixteen, and ain't nobody would of ever believed us we lied about our age. Hell, we lied about our age next year, but by then Bill was almost eighteen and I was so big we told them I was the oldest, nineteen years old, and I reckon they bought it.

Hard for a white guy like you, Connecticut, West Point, all that, hard for you to know what it was like back then in Mississippi for a black man. Medgar Evers, he wasn't nothing

39

but the tip of the damn iceberg. Old Man Barnett was still the Governor. Whew. Piece of work. Remember James Meredith? Malcolm X? Martin Luther King? That little girl over there in Little Rock? Them three kids got themselves killed and buried in that levy over there in Philadelphia? The White Citizens Council? Shit. We used to all the time see them Ku Klux Klan fools in they white sheets standing around recruiting just as natural and relaxed as the Salvation Army at Christmas. Used to see them too in civilian clothes, hanging around on the front porch of every little country store and gas station, hands in they jeans pockets with three fingers hanging out so you'd know, three fingers for three Ks. Lynchings every Saturday night somewhere, seemed like, just for fun, every time them old boys get themselves all liquored up or angered up. Same damn thing. Church bombings. All that, and a whole hell of a lot more that didn't make no newspapers, but was talked about soft and low in the black part of town.

Wasn't a black person in Mississippi back then didn't know somebody been strung up or killed. Your neighbor's uncle, your friend's cousin, somebody's daddy in another town. But sometimes it come closer. It came to our town, and Bill seen it. And when it happen it was Leroy, not much older than Bill. We used to sing with him, me and Bill. Looked like Sugar Ray Robinson, Leroy did, slick and pretty. Played the guitar. Blues. Always talking about how he was going to move up to Memphis, play music up there. They said... Aw, shit, LT. They always said the same damn thing. Leroy 'touched' a white woman. Mississippi back then, that only meant one thing in the world. Maybe he brushed her hand by accident buying something at that store where she worked. Maybe he grab her arm to keep her from falling 'cause she slipped. It don't matter. What Leroy did wrong was be a good-looking young black man with a pretty voice and a guitar in the wrong place at the wrong time. We'd hear about them lynchings and other stuff, people talking low and quiet and scared, and when you a kid, seeing grownups scared is about the scariest thing of all. But see, that's how it worked. They only had to lynch one person and the whole black side of town, every black in the state start talking low and quiet, pulling his head in like an old box turtle. And if you ain't seen it, maybe it's even scarier than if you seen it. Maybe what you hear, what you get told, maybe that's worse than the seeing. I don't know. Bill seen it and I see what he told me and all the stuff he didn't say. Which is worse?

There was a big old tulip poplar in a field about two miles south of town, one of the biggest oldest trees anywhere around, and when the grownups started talking low and quiet Bill snuck on down, staying in the woods. I was sick with the trots, only reason I didn't go. He got to that field, crawled right up to the edge of the trees. There's a bunch of white folks there, sheriff and some others, standing around, cars parked out on the road, and all them just standing there and looking and talking. Someone taking photographs. Laughter one time. Laughter. Leroy hanging there, but they could laugh. Bill hid in the woods, but he could see. He said what they done to that boy's body... Looked like they tried to skin him while he still alive. Cut his tool off and put it in his mouth before they strung him up. Strung him up with barb wire. Rope around the branch, barb wire around his neck, knotted into the rope. Strung him up high. Bill said must have been twenty feet or more, clear up close to the branch. There was a little breeze and Leroy kept rotating, left and right, right and left, slow and gentle, dried blood all down his legs and on his bare feet, little string of dried blood hanging down off one foot. Yeah. Strange fruit. I see it now, what I never saw back then. So soon as we heard about that Civil Rights Act, Bill and me, we decided the Army was just about our only chance, went right on down to sign up.

Lot of black folks back then thought heading up north for work was the way out, Detroit, Chicago, New York City, like that, but me and Bill, we knew what happened to our mama. Mamaw told us. Our Daddy, nobody ever did know what happened to him. He just disappeared. Alive? Dead? No idea. But when we was teenagers just starting to get an itchy foot Mamaw told us about our mama, so the Army seem like a real good deal to us. Shit. No matter how tough it was, it couldn't be no worse than Mississippi. Course, back then nobody ever heard of no Viet Nam.

Things started off just about the way you expect it to for a black man. We wanted to be together, me and Bill, and they told us sure, sure, wouldn't be no problem. But I right away got sent to Benning, and they ship Bill off to Fort Jackson up there in South Carolina.

Sixteen years old and on my own. You black, growing up in Mississippi back then, you learn real quick don't do nothing to draw no attention to yourself. Pull your head in like a terrapin and stay quiet. But when you my size, that ain't always easy. Sixteen years old and I only saw two, three other guys on that whole damn base big as me, and they white. I learned a whole lot about fighting real quick. Every red-necked piece of cracker trash had to try his luck. There was plenty of nights I went to sleep my pillow was pretty damp, but no white man ever knocked me down. All I had to do was think of Leroy. Think of Bill and think of Leroy.

Argentina, Entre Rios Province, 1976

THE BACK ALLÉE, from the house to the stables, was only a few hundred meters long, but the main allée, from the house to the highway, ran as straight as a Roman road for one kilometer before it made a sharp ninety-degree turn for a final three-hundred meters. She had been intrigued by that random and unnecessary turning and had asked Ian about it, but it was something he had grown up with and so never questioned. Perhaps, he had suggested, his grandfather had done it to hide the house from the prying eyes of the world.

The entire length, front and back, was lined with lindens, most old and large, a few new and small replacements for storm-damaged originals, and almost every other tree had a parakeet colony, large and intricate communal nests of sticks, some as big as armoires, that reminded her of old apartment buildings in Buenos Aires, structurally strong and beautiful in the intricacy of their architecture, but shabby and in need of paint. Some of the nests had been taken over by interlopers, mostly teal, amiable squatters raising their young in other people's homes, even though the nearest marsh was almost a mile away and the Uruguay River even farther. The parakeets were noisy birds, each colony warring with its neighbors for... For what? She and Ian had

43

deplored their depredations and the damage to the corn in particular, but no matter what they did, the colonies had endured and increased over the years, so surely there was enough for all. They were clever survivors. In the old days, when Ian was alive, and even before, when his father was still alive, generations of young European men had come to hunt dove and duck and confidently sallied forth to reduce the parakeet numbers, only to return to the house chagrined and wiser. The birds appeared to know what a shotgun was, and to even get a shot was a rare thing, usually done at great distance. Because they were so long-lived, twenty or twenty-five years, they reproduced at a prodigious rate, and now, at the beginning of October with breeding in full swing, the noise they made was so loud and constant it became a sort of background noise she no longer heard or noticed until someone else commented on it.

At the ninety-degree corner she turned and started back. From here the house was invisible through the tunnel of branches, but as she got closer it came into view in gradual stages, bits and pieces that suggested a house—the outer circle of lawn and gravel driveway, then a stone fountain, the broad steps up to the veranda, and finally the front door—long before the house itself could be seen in all its inappropriate European entirety.

She had seen this slow and piecemeal revelation so many times in all the periods of her life: as a child visiting with her parents; as an eager young bride; as a contented wife moving into middle age; and now as an aging widow responsible for dozens of human lives, thousands of cattle, scores of horses, the ancient and arthritic Labrador who walked with her, an unknown number of cats, responsible too for a family tradition represented by the ancestral portraits, hers and Ian's, that hung together throughout the house, reproving Victorians frowning at jovial and probably morally reprehensible Georgians, a formidable, anonymous Jacobean presiding over the dining room in stiff black silk crêpe and stiff black van dyke and a stiff white lace collar that looked as intricate and uncomfortable and fragile as bone china around his neck, paintings and furniture and silver that been preserved and passed on from generation to generation on both sides, a continuum of time and familial history. At sixty-six and childless the question of what to do with it all was beginning to grate on her, a blister of uncertainty and concern. Things she had loved—that she still loved, she still loved!—now carried the oppressive weight of the past and her responsibility to it. The padauk wood bombé chest in which her mother had kept her blouses and nightgowns and that still retained the real or imagined shadow of her scent. It had been brought back from Ceylon by her mother's grandfather. The Peruvian silver ashtray that had always held her father's pipe, a gift from one of his childhood schoolmates, an explorer who vanished searching for something along the vastness of the Ucayali River. Some of these things were valuable, some were not, but all held a link to beloved dead, memories far more precious than the items, and when she died that link, like frayed thread pulled too tight, would break forever. No one else would know. No one else would care. There was a distant cousin she had never met in South Africa, and a distant cousin of Ian's she didn't like in Shropshire, but she could see no reason why either of them would abandon their lives for a ranch in Argentina.

These were the sorts of things she would have loved to discuss with Ian. He would have had a clearer vision of what was right, what was best. He had been wrong about children, in spite of his confident predictions, but he had been right about so many other issues. She didn't know, they never knew, why the barrenness. It was something that couldn't be determined back then. Now she read about "advances," as the magazines put it, "scientific advances," where eggs were counted, sperm were counted, fertility, viability, motility, as if they were so many studs and broodmares, but back then such tests hadn't existed. Such things weren't even discussed, and the result now weighed on her. What to do? Most of their oldest and best friends were either dead or so many years older than she that they soon would be dead. What to do?

Hipólito walked across the circle of driveway and toward her under the trees. At this distance, with his broad shoulders, his baggy *bombachas* and knee-high boots and flat-brimmed *entrerríano* hat, she could almost believe it was his father back from the grave. He even walked with the same small precise steps, as if the absence of a horse beneath him made him mistrustful of the earth he lived on.

"*¿Señora?*" He pulled his hat off and held it by the brim in front of his belly with both hands as his father had done. "*¿Me permite usted una palabra?*"

"*Por supuesto*, Hipólito. What is it?"

She kept walking toward the house, but he didn't follow, and she had to turn around.

"*Señora.*" They were still two hundred yards from the house, but he spoke so softly she took a step back toward him. "A bad thing has happened." He spoke in Spanish. "I think a very bad thing."

"What bad thing, Hipólito?"

"My niece…. You know my sister Patricia and her husband live in La Plata?"

"Yes."

"Her youngest daughter, Reina, has been kidnapped."

"What! Oh, my God. When did this happen?"

"Three weeks ago."

"Have the police not found her?"

"They won't look."

"What do you mean they won't look? That's their job."

"When Patricia told them she had been kidnapped by the Army, the police said such a thing could not happen and they wouldn't do anything. They told Patricia my niece has just run away with a boy, but my brother-in-law's mother, she saw it happen with her own eyes. She swears it was men in army uniforms with army rifles and army trucks."

"The *Army*?"

"Yes, *Señora*."

"Why would the…."

The ancient Lab waddled up and stood smelling Hipólito's hat, his tail beating rhythmically against her thigh.

"How old… Why… What did you say her name was?"

"Reina. Reina Martinez."

"How old is she?"

"Seventeen."

"Was she involved in those protests about the schools and the buses?"

"*Sí*, Señora. Maybe. I think so."

They stood in silence, Hipólito scratching the Lab's ears, the old dog still beating his tail against her leg.

"*Lo siento*. I'm so sorry for your sister, for you, for your family. What would you like me to do?"

"Patricia, my sister, she thought you might be able to speak to General Videla."

"My God, Hipólito, I can't do that. I don't know him. He wouldn't see me. My father knew the General's father-in-law very slightly, but that was forty years ago. He was a professor of something, I think. But I don't know anyone in the junta like that."

The Lab lay down with a little grunt of effort, and Hipólito held his hat with both hands again, turning it slowly by the brim and watching her with the kind of stolid and stoical patience with which he might have watched a young horse, waiting for it to figure out the correct response to pressure.

"I do… I might know one person. I haven't seen him for many years, twenty years, more, but I'll see if I can find him."

He had filled out. The last time she had seen him he was as lean as one of his family's polo ponies and wore a loose white shirt that fluttered when he moved. Now he was, not stout, but substantial and he filled his uniform. The puffy face and white mustache were those of a stranger, but the eyes were the same as he came out of his office to greet her.

"Mrs. Trevelyan, how delightful to see you again after all these years." His English was even better than it had been. "Though looking at you it seems like only twenty-five months, not twenty-five years."

She laughed. "If you're going to lie to my face like that, Colonel, you'd better call me Pamela."

"It is the absolute truth. The hair is grey, as is mine, but you are as beautiful as ever. But yes, please, let's not stand on formalities. You are Pamela, and I am Francisco. Come in. Let's make ourselves comfortable. Will you have coffee?"

They sat in leather chairs in his office and chatted as they waited for an officer who looked about fifteen years old to bring them *café con leche*.

His father had died, but his mother was still alive. Not in the best of health, thank you for asking, in a wheelchair, in fact, but alive and sharp as a fox. Eduardo had lost an eye to a polo ball, and his rating had dropped from nine back down to seven, but even that was a miracle, was it not? Think about the difficulties of depth perception. Extraordinary! Another brother she had never met was killed almost twenty years ago when a horse rolled over him. They still played at La Perdida, but he personally did not get to play as often anymore because of his duties. The older he got, the less time there was in the day, and now all these problems with the terrorists, the subversives, attacking the very businesses and industries that kept the country solvent. Last month the offices of Mercedes, Fiat, Chevrolet, and now poor Carlos Roberto Souto. Did Pamela know him? With Chrysler? Ah, such a good man. It was absurd. Here's our coffee.

They waited in smiling silence until the young officer closed the door.

"What may I do for you, Pamela? Is everything well? Are you in need of anything?"

"When my husband died that day at La Perdida–"

"Such a tragedy, so sad."

"–do you remember the groom who came down with us from *El Rincón*?"

He shook his head and shrugged, his epaulettes adding emphasis to the movement.

"You and he both held me in your arms and you both helped me back to the house."

"Ah. Yes. I do remember. A remarkable face, a face with great character. A young boy. Well, not now, of course. He must be middle-aged."

"Yes. He's worried about his niece. She has disappeared."

"Disappeared? You mean she has run away?"

"No. She was kidnapped."

"Oh, my God. He must go to the police. This is a police matter."

"The family did, but the police won't do anything."

"Why not?"

"Because an eyewitness, a family member who saw the kidnapping, swears the girl was kidnapped by the Army."

Colonel Francisco Alejandro Pieres turned slightly in his chair and put his cup and saucer down on a side table. He put his hands together as if in prayer, fingertips just touching his chin, and looked at her with eyes that revealed only sadness and concern.

"Pamela," he said at last, "These are very difficult times. Argentina—more: the whole southern cone of South America, even Brazil—is under attack, but what makes it so difficult is that it is not a single enemy. If we were at war with, oh, Paraguay, that would be a clearly defined antagonist. We would fight—we would win, I have no doubt—but we would fight knowing who we fought, who we had to overcome, and how we had to fight. This attack, this war we are now engaged in—and yes, it is a war—is one unlike any ever fought before in the history of the world. We fight many adversaries, internal and external, with many different goals and agendas. We lump them all under the name of left wing subversives, but they are radicals of every shape and color: Marxists, Leninists, Peronists, anti-Peronists, Guevarists, trade unionists, students, communists, priests, Catholics, Jews, all with different ideologies, all with different objectives. Sometimes they work together, sometimes they fight each other. It is a mess, a confused but very dangerous mess, and we, you and I and all who support Argentina, we have to do what must be done.

"Now, having said all that, I can assure you the Army is not in the business of kidnapping people. We arrest subversives and terrorists and extremists, and we wipe them out when and where we can, but we do not kidnap."

"And the aunt or the grandmother or whoever it was who saw the kidnapping…?"

The epaulettes rose and fell. "I have no doubt she saw men in army uniforms, but who were they? Montoneros? The ERP, how do you call them in English, the People's Revolutionary Army? Remember Azul, when they attacked the barracks dressed as soldiers? Camilo, Colonel Camilo Gay and his wife Hilda, did you know them? They were lovely people. They did not deserve to die at the hands of those barbarians. That is what we face, Pamela. And worse. Bombs in hotels and movie theaters and businesses. And for what? Do you know what they want? I'll tell you: chaos. It's that simple. They believe, the ERP especially, they have a theory that a government, any government, can be overthrown if they can create the impression of chaos. My God, what morons! Do they think they have to create an impression of chaos with inflation at two hundred percent or three hundred percent or whatever it is today? There is chaos enough for everyone without their nonsense."

"Is it possible she was arrested by the Army?"

"It is possible she was arrested and there has been some breakdown in communication. That is possible. Anything is possible. As I said, we don't need the ERP to create chaos for us. We can do it very well by ourselves. Give me her name, this girl, and her age, address, any information you have, and I will make inquiries. I make no promises, but I will make inquiries. For you, for the memory of your husband, and for your young groom who is not so young anymore."

Los Angeles, 1982

VIET NAM. VIET NAM! No way I could of ever dreamed nothing like that. Viet Nam. All them woods down there in Mississippi look like open fields next to Viet Nam. Jungle. Just that word make your heart go a little faster. Woods is thick and there's deer in there and all like that, but jungle... Jungle something different, something scary. Bad things in a jungle. Snakes, toe poppers, what they call them mosquito mines, bouncing betties, punji sticks, gooks, all that stuff you can't see but you know is there.

I don't think any man ever born, black or white or yellow or any other damn color ever forget the first man he kill. They teach you how to kill, that's all you do, that's what you spend all that time training for, but they can't train you what the reality is. I mean how it really is. How it is before, how it is while you're doing it, how it is after, looking at what you just done. There ain't no training can teach you that, and there ain't no forgetting.

We was all spread out all over the damn place, and I'm walking on this trail, not much more than what a deer trail would be like back home, jungle on both sides thicker than you can believe possible. You can't see nothing. There could be anything in there, gooks, tigers, houses, hell you never know it. Can't see any damn thing more than about ten feet in on either side of you, Lieutenant. And I'm walking along this little teeny trail, come around a curve and bang! There he is, just standing there. First Viet Cong I ever saw. I'm standing there in my uniform, holding my M-16, my M-16A1 5.56mm assault rifle, Sir! I got a Colt M1911.45 on my hip, I got enough damn ammo to wipe out a good-sized town, I got hand grenades and all kinds of stuff hanging off of me, I'm big as a damn mountain, I'm a trained killer, trained to react instantly and lethally—that's what they tell us, how they say it—trained by the best damned instructors in the best damned army in the history of the whole damned world, and I just stand there looking at him. He's in his black pajamas, no bigger than a kid, holding his rifle, a damn M1, looking up at me.

I seen gooks before, and I thought I knew what to expect, what they look like and all, them little slanty eyes, but this kid, he look about twelve years old, a twelve-year-old girl, a small twelve-year-old girl, he's standing there looking up at me, probably never seen nothing so big and ugly his whole damn life, and his eyes is as big and round as garbage can lids. I imagine mine was too. And we just stand there looking at each other. Felt like an hour back then. Now, I look back and remember, and it seems like we stood and just looked at each other all afternoon, maybe a whole damned day.

Funny thing, Lieutenant, something nobody talked about all that time they training us to be killers. You split in two. Right there, right then, you ain't one person anymore. You two people, maybe more and it's like those two people or three or however many you suddenly become, it's like they almost talking to each other even as they're all thinking about completely different things and seeing different things and hearing different things.

And that's the first thing: there ain't no sound anymore. That jungle, it's noisy as hell when there ain't nobody around, but it gets real quiet when there's people in there, but that quiet ain't nothing next to the quiet while I'm standing there looking at this little kid. There just ain't no sound anywhere in the whole damn world. It's that quiet. And part of me is thinking about that quiet. And another part of me, the Army part, the trained killer part, he's thinking, "I got to kill this guy." But same time, some other part of me thinking, "This is just the most natural thing in the whole damn world, two guys meeting each other walking through the woods like this; we ought to say a few words, pass the time of day, then each of us go on our way. That's what folks do when they meet up with each other somewhere, someplace, be polite." And then the Army part of me, or maybe some other part is thinking, "I can't kill no little kid," but even while I'm thinking that and thinking all them other things, I'm thinking about the mechanics of it, all the stuff I been trained to do that I ain't even supposed to think about, just supposed to do it automatically. You know, swing the barrel of the rifle up to cover the target, move your finger onto the trigger, all the physical stuff you practiced back there in Georgia, the stuff you practiced over and over so's you wouldn't never have to think about it, just do it natural, a part of you is standing there thinking about what you ain't even supposed to think about.

So after a couple of hours I start swinging the muzzle up, and it's like it some kind of damned dance, something me and this little kid practiced, worked on together, cause he start swinging his muzzle up. And we still just staring at each other. My shirt sticking to me with sweat in the back, but it's kind of pooched out in the front some and the tip of the butt end of my stock, the toe, catches on the shirt just a little and I'm thinking, "That ain't good." But even before that thought can finish traipsing across my mind another thought, or maybe one of those other guys I split into, says, "Don't make no never mind," cause I already bulled through and my finger's on the trigger and before I even know what I'm doing I've emptied half a magazine.

Why? What for? One bullet would of killed that little kid deader than an anvil. Wasn't no need to waste all them bullets, but I guess I was a whole lot more scared than I knew or thought or felt, cause blip, they gone, all them bullets hitting right in the thoracic cavity. See what all I learned in the army, what they taught me, fancy words and everything? All of them bullets packed together tighter than the palm of my hand, every one of them hitting him before that kid even had time to fall. That's how scared I was and I didn't even know it.

Next thing I know there's voices everywhere, people yelling, some of them calling my name, and then there's people all around me, pounding me on the back laughing, congratulating me like I done something good or brave, like I'm some kind of damned hero for shooting a bunch of bullets into some little kid I could of busted in two.

That was my first.

After that it gets easier and easier until at last, towards the end, you don't kill cause of no anger or hate or righteousness or any kind of feeling, not love, not even fear. Nothing like that. You only kill cause you tired, too damn tired to do anything else. "Infinite fatigue," what you white college boys called it. You kill because you too damn tired to care anymore, to make no decisions as to right or wrong, good or bad, friend or enemy. You see someone, maybe someone right in your platoon, maybe even someone you think of as a friend, you see them doing something you know going to get themselves killed deader than dirt, and you know it's your damn responsibility as a sergeant and as a fellow soldier, it's your responsibility to stop them, all you got to do is sing out, but you so damn tired you can't get your brain to send the words to your mouth in time. I seen it happen. I done it. Let it happen. Or maybe there's someone, some gook walking along, and that gook he could be old or young, man or woman, it didn't make no never mind. It just mean making decisions, effort, responsibility, doing something, when all you want to do is sleep, and so you kill cause you so damned tired, because killing is easier than not killing. So tired.

That was Viet Nam, Lieutenant, the Viet Nam you never lived long enough to see and know. All them dead people was enemies; twelve-year-old boy soldiers, little bitty girls maybe eight years old, eighty-year-old women, ancient men hobbling along all bent over they bamboo sticks; it don't matter. When they dead, it don't matter no more; the dead, they all enemies.

Even you, Lieutenant. Even you.

Argentina, Buenos Aires Province, 1977

WHEN SHE WAS A GIRL, the Hurlingham Club was still in open country and reminded her of a more masculine version of Whitfield Old Hall, an uncompromising, English only, wood-paneled tribute to the traditions and faded elegance of the British Empire, an oasis of cricket and squash and lawn tennis as well as polo. The club was not named for the town. The town, now a suburb of Buenos Aires, was named for the club it grew up around, and the club was named after the original polo club in London. Ian had been a member, as had her father, but after her husband's death she had resigned her membership as neither geographically nor economically practical. This was the first time she had been there in almost ten years.

An adjutant, possibly the fifteen-year-old who brought in the *café con leche*, had called on behalf of Colonel Francisco Pieres. The Colonel extended his apologies for not calling personally, but an emergency had come up and he had been called to Bahia Blanca. The Colonel wanted her to know that his brother Eduardo would be playing at Hurlingham and perhaps she might like to watch the game as she had played against him herself. There would be an invitation and a pass waiting for her.

That was all. There was no mention of Reina Martinez or Hipólito or any information that might have been learned, or even if Francisco would be there. Just an invitation to a polo game.

The club had moved forward with the times. There were as many Argentinean members as there were British, and the English-language-only rule had given way to the charming bilingual confusion of upper-class Argentina. The young men and women were slim and elegant and exquisitely fashionable, shockingly beautiful, with the *café con leche* skin and masses of black hair that came from a melting pot of breeding, golden hair and blue eyes belonging to people who spoke not a word of English, all with the grace and confidence that came with wealth and privilege. Old friends, who had also once been shockingly beautiful, greeted her with surprise and delight, as if she had returned from a long journey, and their aging bodies and graying hair reminded her how much she had withdrawn from the world since Ian's death.

She found Eduardo, still as lean as a fence post and almost unchanged but for grey hair and a black eye patch, but he didn't know where Francisco was or even if he was there at all. Was she still playing polo? She must come back and play again at La Perdida. He had some horses he thought might interest her.

She watched the game with the mixture of excitement and envy common to all who watch a game they love played by others. Between the chukkas she stood and looked for Francisco, but there was no sign of him. She caught up with friends, talked horses with people she had played with and against, and beef prices with other Anglo-Argentine ranchers, but she saw no one in uniform.

At halftime she went out onto the field with the other spectators to stomp down the divots. Scattered cumulus clouds were blowing in from the east offering moving pockets of temporary cool. She had her head down and was trying to flip over a clod of grass and earth with the toe of her shoe when Francisco appeared beside her. He was in mufti, quartered away from her, concentrating on divots, and spoke softly and quickly in English.

"Do not look at me. Pretend you have nothing to do with me. Do not look, Pamela. Turn away, turn away quickly." He bent down to pick up a clump of grass and replaced it in a divot. "Things are getting bad, Pamela, very bad and your questions could not have come at a worse time, for you or for me. They have arrested Bob Cox of the Buenos Aires Herald, and because of him they are looking at everyone of British descent. You are all considered suspect at best and enemies at worst. Because you asked about that child, you are now being watched, every action, everyone you talk to. You must be very careful what you say and who you say it to. If they think you are trying to help the left, anyone on the left, however little, you will be arrested. As long as you do nothing to provoke them they don't dare touch you. I mean all you English. But if they can take Cox, they will take anyone. Because I asked questions on your behalf I am now, how do you say, under a cloud and I must go very hard the other way to get out. Be very careful, Pamela. Go back to your estancia and stay as quiet and small as possible. Goodbye."

Out of the corner of her eye she saw him walk away, moving from divot to divot back into the heavier press of people near the center of the field.

Los Angeles, 1982

I DIDN'T HAVE NOTHING AGAINST YOU, Lieutenant. Hell, you one of the few white men I ever met wasn't no racist. At least not no more than any white boy grows up rich and educated and knowing he's better and smarter and richer than everyone who ain't just like him. But you wasn't a bad guy. You was just young and dumb and scared. Older than me, but years and years younger, coming out of Connecticut and West Point and all, the way you was raised. You couldn't help it.

You remember? That's my damn problem, LT. I can't forget. I remember all the dead.

I remember they faces. I remember they names. Cooper, Joey Cooper, nasty little weasel out of California. Rodriquez, Ernesto Rodriquez, Phoenix Arizona. Michael Parrot, Iowa. Richie Lawless, Nebraska. Sam Jankowski, Seattle Washington. Bernie Schwartz, Paterson New Jersey. Newton the Newt Oldmann, Pensacola Florida... Lots more. Lots more. All of them my kids, my boys, my sons, the sons I never had, ain't never going to have. I liked some of them better than others, some of them I didn't like at all one little bit, but they all my sons.

And I remember Lieutenant James Samuel Legendre Catton, New Haven, Connecticut, West Point, class of '68, daddy West Point before you, orthopedic surgeon right there in New Haven, older brother, polio. I thought about that older brother a whole bunch, Lieutenant, and how it got pushed onto you, all that carrying it forward, all that tradition and shit, cause I could tell before more than ten words come out of your mouth that the army, soldiering, West Point, none of that come natural to you. Be like putting hames and traces on a thoroughbred and asking him to pull stumps out of bottom land. I think about that older brother now, wonder what he thinking when he think about you. He take on a bunch of guilt for that gimpy leg or arm or whatever it was kept him home and safe? Think about your daddy, the Major, and I wonder what folks with four names think and feel when they son get his head blowed off. Guilt? Pride? When folks like that dream at night, how do they dream about you? They see some skinny little boy in his gray and white uniform throwing his hat in the air with all them other little boys? They see the boy who somehow graduated seventh in his class, or they see you so scared you shaking with fear underneath a little dike at the bottom of a paddy, sending boys out to die over and over 'cause you too scared to think? Or do they maybe see some other little boy, five, eight, ten years old, laughing, riding a bike, playing baseball, some little boy who should of growed up to be a doctor or a lawyer or some such? I don't know what folks like you think and dream.

My dreams... All I tell you, Lieutenant, is my good dreams is the ones when I dream of Bill lying in his grave back there in South Carolina somewheres and I wake up crying. Them's the good dreams.

Wasn't your fault, Lieutenant. Wasn't none of our fault. God knows you tried, but can't none of us be anything other than what we are. And I didn't know what else to do. If I took over command, you'd of been in the right if you blowed my head off. Best I could of hoped for was being busted back down to private. What else could I done?

I tried to tell you it was too quiet when we come out around that little hill. Too quiet on that rise. Too quiet in the jungle. Too quiet everywhere. I tried. You learn what's right and normal and what ain't. Even if you ain't been somewhere long enough to know, if you a natural born soldier, got soldier there inside you just as part of what you born with, you don't need to be anywhere too long. You just know. You come around a bend, you walk into a house, you start moving down a street some little village somewhere, walk into a room, whatever, and bang! That warning go off, a neon sign dropping down right there in front of you. It goes off, that neon sign thing in your head, that alarm, it goes off and you know, you know something ain't right. You see that neon sign, it say maybe "Danger," or "Look out," or "Go back," whatever it say to you, and it don't mean somebody got his gun on you already, but it mean somebody fixing to put crosshairs on you next street, next bend, next room, next step. I felt it and I saw it, saw my neon sign, and I tried to tell you. I showed you there wasn't nobody doing no work any of them paddies.

What we should of done, we should of dropped back down that little bit of road, gone through around the backside of that rise, that little hill thing. More work, more slogging, but then we'd of been in good position. Well, as good as anything can be in Nam. We should of done that. Wasn't no damn stopwatch on us or nothing.

Book learning's a fine thing, Lieutenant, but it ain't the same thing as real learning. Ain't the same thing by a long damn stretch. Some things you can't learn except by doing, by being there.

Ricky Chapman, Llano, Texas. First guy to go down, almost before we even heard the shots, before the sound travel across that damn paddy, he's down with his whole throat just shot away, grabbing at hisself, trying to keep his own self alive. And we all diving down behind that little piece of dike.

Never forget the smell of dirt over there. Different. Not like dirt here in Los Angeles or Mississippi or Georgia. Dirt here, it smells like life, like things going to grow. Over there it always smelled like metal, like shit, like death, like blood soaked into the ground. You maybe grow stuff over there, rice and all, but that dirt smell like death.

We're down, hugging the ground behind that little paddy dike, listening to they guns, the bullets going over our heads, everybody yelling, Karl Sanger screaming on his radio, Ricky Chapman gurgling to death, all of it, and I knew right away they was a whole bunch of gooks over there, other side of that paddy. I tried to tell you, LT. I tried, but I could tell before the first word come out of my mouth you was gone. You was in panic mode, your brain going so code red you couldn't think. You start screaming about how we got to get to that next dike, got to charge across to that next dike, and all I could think was, Charge? What the hell you mean charge? What the hell for? Even we make it, we only going to be a little bit closer and then we just be lying in water. Where's the good in that?

But you couldn't hear me. I lying right next to you, right there beside you, yelling into your left ear, yelling, telling you what we had to do, how we got to do it so we could get them sons of bitches, telling you what I knew to do and how to do, yelling. I tried. But you couldn't hear me. All you could hear was your own fear.

Them first five boys you sent? Not one of them made as far as I could throw a hand grenade. Hell, I could of thrown a damn M60 as far as they made it. Every one of them dead before they faces hit the water.

And I'm yelling, screaming, pleading with you, begging, telling you I can do it, I can do it, but that fear, fear like that it make a man deaf. I wonder sometimes if LeRoy even heard what all those white folks say to him before they kill him, or if fear made him deaf too. It's a big thing, fear.

Then you sent them next five. They didn't make it far as the first bunch. It was Bernie Schwartz made me see what I had to do. Funny thing is, I didn't like him, Bernie Schwartz, Paterson, New Jersey. Conceited little stuck-up son of a bitch, all the time bragging about how many damn girls sick in love with him, flexing his damn little useless muscles, strutting around with his shirt off ever chance he got. Useless little piece of crap. But it was him. He kept trying to stand up, like he was going keep on going, get to them damn gooks if he had take a bullet every step he take. And he did. They keep shooting him, he keep falling down, getting up and yelling and trying to move and they keep shooting and there's blood coming out him like some kind of damn fountain in front of the county courthouse. And I knew then.

I remember it all like it something I seen someone else do, pulling my sidearm out, finger down the slide, thumb up there on the safety, bringing it up, no rush, no hurry, barrel right there on the side of you cheekbone, just below the temple, safety off, finger to the trigger, barrel angled up. I didn't want that bullet to go right through and kill Karl Sanger over there on your right side.

What I wonder about most is what you thought then, what you thought in that—what was it?—quarter second maybe between feeling my barrel cool and hard angling up against you cheekbone and then feeling nothing again ever. What you think about in that little bitty space of time? How many thoughts went through you head before the bullet went through? Did the fear stop? Was there just a flash, a little piece of a second, when you knew how bad you screwed up, all them boys dead out there in the water? Did you know? Did you understand? Did you see why, what I had to do and why?

I tried to tell you, Lieutenant. I tried.

Part II

Argentina, Entre Rios Province, 1978

THE MARE SHE RODE WAS NAMED RISADA and she was twenty-two years old, still sound, but too old for serious competition. Of course, at sixty-eight Pamela felt herself too old for serious competition as well. She still played—not on Risada—but not as often or as seriously as she had forty years ago or thirty or even twenty years ago, back when Arturo Mora had presented the mare to her, a bony, nondescript bay with a head like a hammer and a neck that hovered on the brink of ewe-shaped. Risada—and why had anyone named a horse 'Laughter?'—had been intended as a courting gift, a graceful and subtle and well-chosen way for Arturo to express his desires, as some more inelegant man might have presented her with diamonds. Any horse would have meant more to her than diamonds, but Risada had proved her worth over and over again, with sweetness of disposition and the kind of speed, agility, and heart of the greatest champions. Pamela had turned Arturo down, but if he had demanded his gift back, she would have married him just to keep the mare.

Now, after almost twenty years together, she and the mare loped lazily around on the practice field near the stables, hitting the hard wooden ball, forehand, backhand, near-side, off-side, tail shot, neck shot, the old mare's easy canter softening the impact on Pamela's stiffening spine, her gentle shots asking little of the horse, mallet hand and shoulder already protesting.

"We're two old ladies, you and I."

The mare's ears flicked back at the sound of her voice.

It had taken her a long time to reconcile herself with aging. Not the fact of it, not the grey hair, the skin creased and wrinkled from a lifetime spent outside, the thickening of her body, not even the multiple aches and pains. It was the disparity between perception and reality: she looked out at the world with the heart of a young woman, but she mounted a horse with the stiffened knees of age; the hand that held the mallet now was her mother's hand.

She hit the ball a final time, driving it back toward the stables and was gratified to see it stop almost precisely where she had wanted it. She walked Risada slowly around the circumference of the field, giving her time to breathe and cool down. Hipólito would hand-walk the mare as soon as she stepped off, but the chance to do nothing but walk quietly was good for both old ladies.

Hipólito wasn't at the stable. She called his name twice, something she had never had to do before, but there was no response. She slipped the bridle off and the mare immediately dropped her head and began to graze. She took the bridle into the tack room, the best-smelling room in the world, leather and horse and saddle soap, and went back out. She pulled up the stirrups and undid the girth and pulled the saddle off. As she turned around Hipólito stepped out of one of the stalls in the back and she knew, not even able to see his face clearly in the shadows, but she knew something was very wrong.

"*Señora.*"

She stood the saddle on its end at the door to the tack room and walked to him. Saying nothing, he turned his head, looking into the stall.

She expected an injured horse, perhaps, brought in from one of the pastures, perhaps a mare in labor and distress, or a stillborn foal, though she hadn't bred a horse in nearly a decade.

It was a teenaged girl she had never seen before, little more than a child, skeletal, unbathed, crouched in the shavings, a dirty cotton dress, bare feet in filthy unlaced tennis shoes, scratches on her legs as if she had pushed through brambles, and in her eyes the feral, terrified look of an animal of prey.

She understood, but it took a moment for the name to come back to her.

"It's her, your niece from La Plata. Reina."

"*No, Señora.*"

"No?"

"*No.*"

"Who is she?"

Hipólito didn't answer. Instead, he looked at the girl. "*Dígale.*"

The girl said nothing. She stared at Pamela, as frozen as a rabbit.

"Tell me your name, child." She spoke in Spanish as softly as she might to a four year old. "*¿Comó te llamas?*"

"Candelas."

"And how do you come to be here? Who brought you here?"

"I walked."

"From where?"

"Near Buenos Aires."

"That's not possible. It's over two hundred kilometers."

The girl said nothing.

"You *walked*? How long did you walk to get here?"

The girl made an almost imperceptible movement with her shoulders that might have been a shrug. "A month, maybe more."

"Where did you sleep? Where did you eat if you walked all that way? And why? Why did you come here? What's going on?"

She looked at Hipólito to include him in the last question, but he never took his eyes off the girl. Instead, he said again, "*Dígale.*" He spoke as he might to a terrified horse. "*Dígale.*"

For the first time the girl looked away, into a corner of the stall and never took her eyes off that spot while she spoke, as if she were recounting events played before her on a television screen, her voice quiet and dusty and completely monotone, no inflection, no emotion, a child reading badly from a book filled with words she neither comprehended nor cared to understand.

She was fifteen, but only one year behind Reina in school. They weren't friends, but friendly, and she had joined Reina and the others in the protests. They did no harm, chanting and singing and laughing. It was a lark, it was fun. They meant no harm.

A week later she was in the kitchen with her mother. They were singing along with the radio. Her mother sang always, with her, with the radio, quietly under her breath as she shopped or waited for the bus, as she cooked or cleaned or washed. Always she sang, and they were singing together like two girls when the army burst into her family's apartment. The soldiers grabbed her and her brother, and when her father tried to stop them they beat him unconscious. Her mother stood in the kitchen, screaming, with her hands over her ears as if she were trying to muffle the sound of her own screams, pleading with them not to hurt her husband. The army dragged them all down the stairs, but because her father was unconscious they dragged him by his feet, and his head hit each step, thump, thump, thump, leaving a little smear of blood on each tread.

They were blindfolded and put in the back of a truck. She thought there must have been other prisoners too because she could hear a woman weeping who was not her mother. They were told if they ever even attempted to remove the blindfolds, ever, they would be killed immediately. They were taken to a place somewhere just outside Buenos Aires. Later, another prisoner told her it was an army base or barracks.

It began that night. In a room in the barracks they were forced to kneel. Then each one had to say his name, so even though she was blindfolded, she knew her father and mother and brother were there, and others too, perhaps unable to see, but able to listen. She didn't know how many men raped her. Many. Her mother too. But they did something more to her mother because at one point her screams went from one register to another, a shriek of greater intensity, a horrible parody of musical scales, rising and rising, the singing voice lowering only to beg, and once a note of outrage, almost anger or disbelief, then rising again, rising and rising in agony. She didn't know what they did to her father and brother, but when the soldiers were done with her and her mother and the other woman, she could hear their screams too, in their turn. She could still hear them. She never saw her family again. Not 'saw,' because she couldn't see. She never heard their voices again. But she still heard their screams. She still heard the beloved voice rising though the scales and beyond.

She was put in a room with other prisoners. Most were strangers, but two were students from her school. One was Reina. They were all blindfolded and chained. For many weeks, she wasn't sure how many, perhaps months, she never saw anything. They learned, the prisoners, to use their ears to determine when guards were in the room with them, and when they were alone they would whisper back and forth, try to pass information, encouragement, hope. Hope without belief. If their ears deceived them, whoever spoke was beaten.

She discovered over the days or weeks or months, that rape was a welcome relief from torture. Because she was young and the soldiers thought her pretty, she was raped more often than tortured, but she felt enough of the other to know. They used a cattle prod and something worse, something they called *la margarita*, that had more volts. It varied. Sometimes they stuck wires under her toenails and finger nails and gave her the shock there. Sometimes they attached electrodes, like the end of a battery cable, to her nipples. Sometimes they put it under her armpits or on her tongue, the soles of her feet, in her vagina, in her anus. They would throw water on her to increase the intensity of the shocks. Whether she was raped or tortured depended on who the soldiers were that day. At first they wanted names of other students, protesters. Towards the end they just wanted fun. She didn't know how long it went on, days or weeks or months, because the frame of reference of the tortured changes from time to pain. There is agony and there is worse. That is all there is.

In the whispered conversations of perpetual dark she learned there were other tortures, additional tortures for the men. Sometimes they were buried alive in pits, naked, with just their heads exposed, in the heat and rain, without food and water, as the insects under the ground ate their flesh, until they talked or died. The soldiers didn't seem to care which. Some of the men would be electrocuted on the soles of their feet, or have the bones in their feet broken with a hammer, and then they were forced to stand with a thin wire tied tight around their testicles and to the bars of the window, so that when they collapsed they would castrate themselves. The soldiers used to bet on this, wagering money and cigarettes on how long it would take. All this and more she learned whispering in the dark.

One day Reina didn't come back and she learned later from another prisoner that the soldiers had used too much electricity.

She escaped by accident. They took all the prisoners who were still alive in her cell outside and told them to get onto a truck, they were going to be flown somewhere on an airplane. But because she was still blindfolded she stumbled into a ditch and fell. She was struggling to get up when she realized no one was beating her, so she lay still. Apparently they never missed her because she heard the truck start up and drive away. When she finally dared to take her blindfold off the sun was so intense she couldn't see after so many weeks of darkness, so she stayed where she was until night and then walked away. One of the prisoners had told her to go to Uruguay, but not directly across the river near Buenos Aires, because there were soldiers watching everywhere, but to go north first. Reina had told her about *El Rincón* and her uncle who worked for an English lady, so she had come here. She wanted to get across the river to Uruguay.

Hipólito took her across the river in the little boat they had used once to take their guests duck hunting. They gave her food and clothes and money and directions to a town where she said she had a friend. Pamela went down to the boathouse by the marsh and watched them push off, the ancient outboard coughing and spewing like a chronic smoker.

Did she know? Did she have a premonition of what was to come? She must have, because a few days later she bought a new engine for the little boat, and less than two months after that it began to earn its keep.

What she did not know was whether it was Candelas or Hipólito or some other even more tenuous word of mouth—words whispered in the dark—but whoever or however it was done, they began to come.

The first was another girl, fortunate enough to have been tipped off to avoid arrest. Then there was a girl who had been arrested and tortured, but only for a few days before she was released. Then came a man and his wife, the man so severely tortured his gums and testicles were both suppurating and he was only able to walk supported by his wife. It finally averaged out to about two a month, though once there was an entire family of seven, including a grandmother, and Hipólito had to ferry them across in two shifts. They came on foot, in cars, on bicycles, once in a farm cart drawn by a three-up. They came from Buenos Aires, from Córdoba, from Santa Fe, from Tucumán, even once all the way up from Viedma, and each brought with him a tessera of evil so that by the end she had a mosaic of the unspeakable, of mass graves, of disappearances, of the living being thrown out of airplanes into the Atlantic, of the arbitrary extermination of a people, the extermination of a way of thinking.

She wondered what her husband would have thought, what her father and mother would have thought. She couldn't imagine, but she knew what each of them would have done, and she did it. She felt a wave of nausea each time Hipólito signaled to her, nodding his head in the direction of one of the disused cabins beyond the stable where once as a baby he had danced in his mother's arms and where the mother still lived, dressed in black, a widow now for longer even than old Petra had been. She felt the wave of nausea, but she would go to the little safe in her bedroom and take some money, have some food prepared, and do what had to be done.

Argentina, Entre Rios Province, 1981

THE KNOCK ON HER BEDROOM DOOR came as no surprise. She was drifting in and out of the fitful half-sleep of the elderly when she heard Hipólito running up the stairs and came wide awake with a burst of adrenaline.

"¡Señora!"

Someone had called him. He didn't say who—perhaps he didn't know—but the army was on its way, had already passed through the tiny village of Las Moscas, he didn't know how long ago, but they were close, very close. For God's sake hurry, *Señora*.

She had known this might happen. She hadn't allowed herself to think about it, she hadn't allowed herself to believe it would, but she had known, had accepted it on some level as a possibility even when she watched Candelas, frail and filthy, hunched over in the little boat, her life destroyed before it was begun, vanishing on the far side of the river.

She had an ancient canvas backpack, a remnant of the early days of her marriage, on a shelf in her closet. The few clothes she grabbed were sturdy and practical. She didn't need much because it would only be a matter of days, or weeks at most, before things calmed down and she would be able to return. Her passport and money were in the little safe.

When they went down the stairs, instead of turning toward the back entrance, she went into the library.

Why? She never knew. Was it for the papers she kept in her desk? There was nothing so vital she couldn't live without it or replace it eventually. Did she want a book? Did she want to smell once more the room that reminded her so much of Ian? Did she realize on some level she would never see that room again? She didn't know.

She went in. She had her hand on the chain of the old cloisonné standing lamp, but before she could pull it, even as Hipólito cried out, "¡No, *Señora!*" there was a faint flash of reflected light on the ceiling and she moved in the dark to the window and saw the glow of truck lights, ghostly through the leaves, coming around the ninety-degree angle of the drive, coming down the long allée of lindens, driving methodically, without hurry, inexorably, an army on the move.

"¡*Dése prisa, Señora! ¡Por Dios!*"

She couldn't possibly keep up with Hipólito, so he took her backpack in one hand and her arm in the other and ran with her. He was fantastically strong, and whenever she stumbled he kept her from falling, dragging her, pulling her, lifting her, so that sometimes she felt almost airborne.

They were on the other side of the barn, running past the old cabins, when they heard voices behind them at the house, and they had already turned onto the lane that led to the boathouse before the first trucks drove to the barn and there were more voices, shouting commands, a crash, a curse, a sound of breaking glass. Even in her fear she had to stifle an urge to return, to confront them, to order them off her property. How dare they! How dare they damage her property, things sacred to her with the memories of Ian and her father and mother, sacred with the weight of the beloved and vanished past, sacred too in the unbroken line of succession back to a more distant past? For the first time she understood how and why that unknown maternal ancestor had thrown herself off the battlements.

Hipólito threw her pack into the boat and put the oars in and pushed her off, whispering even though they were several hundred yards away. "Don't start the engine, *Señora*, not even out on the river. The sound will carry. Go, go! *Vaya con Dios*."

The night was very dark, and the fog that would lie on the marshes and the river in the morning was already beginning to thicken, so she was both protected and hampered. Even with the outboard it would have been hard to follow the channel through to the river, but rowing, facing backward, she ran aground again and again, each time having to stand and push herself free with an oar and start over.

It was slow going. Once she found herself completely surrounded by land in what she thought was the right direction and she had to turn around and row back toward danger to find the channel again, but she never saw the feared lights, nor heard any sound of a boat engine in pursuit. Perhaps they hadn't counted on her using a boat. Perhaps they hadn't counted on her being warned. She kept on, alternately rowing and punting, until at last she could feel the current and was able to row freely and consistently, and knew she was out on the Uruguay River.

The current proved stronger than she had realized. At this point, in the lowlands between Entre Ríos Province on the Argentine side and the Paysandu Province—or possibly the Río Negro, she wasn't sure—on the Uruguayan side, the river was very wide and looked slow and sluggish, but she could feel herself being carried along. The arthritis in her wrists and right shoulder throbbed in protest and from time to time she had to stop and rest, and each time she became aware again of the current carrying her south toward Buenos Aires and Army barracks and something called *la margarita.*

When she reached the Uruguayan side there was the broad sandy beach that was typical of long stretches of the river, and she knew her boat would be spotted and possibly reported. It took great effort and almost more strength than she had left, and several times the handle of the starter rope pulled out of her hand, but at last she got the little engine running and headed north. She was so far away from *El Rincón* that even if the motor was heard she might pass for a local fisherman getting an early start. Besides, no one would expect her to head back the way she had come. She told herself all these things and prayed they were true.

She passed two little creeks too shallow for her to navigate before she found a small river and headed inland. Night had shifted into the first dim gray light and gray fog of morning, a colorless, featureless, unknown world. The only place in Uruguay she had ever been, years ago with Ian, was Montevideo, and she had no intention of going that close to Buenos Aires. Other than that she was too exhausted to formulate any intention beyond sleeping, and as soon as she found a sapling strong enough to tie off to, she ran the boat onto the sand and made it fast. She spread the life vests on the floor of the boat to make an uncomfortable, lumpy mattress and put her pack under head to make an uncomfortable, lumpy pillow, and fell instantly asleep.

She woke because of the heat, sticky with sweat. It was full sun shining down on her and the air was full of the familiar sounds of home: parakeets squabbling, a duck calling a warning somewhere, doves. Then there was a splash and she sat up. A fish had jumped, the ripples spreading and dispersing in the current. The land around her was familiar but different too, sandy instead of marshy.

She took her pack and walked along the bank of the little tributary to the edge of the Uruguay River and studied the Argentine shore, but she saw nothing familiar. It was impossible to tell how far down the current had carried her or how far back up she had motored in the dark. She was as sore as if she had been thrown from a horse, very thirsty, very hungry, and with no idea of where she was. She walked back past her boat, inland along the tributary, walking sometimes on a sandy bank, sometimes clambering over roots and through brambles. She wondered if the scratches on her legs looked like Candelas'.

Eventually she came to a two-track that forded the little river and she turned to the north. The only tracks were from cattle and horses, and that made her feel safe. After several kilometers the brush gave way to a large pasture where cattle grazed, raising their heads briefly to look at her as they chewed, but there was no sign of a house and on the far side the brush closed around her again. Then she came to another, much larger pasture with more cattle, and on the far edge, riding along the trees, was a gaucho on a sturdy little criollo with a very young colt trotting free behind. She was about to call and wave when he spotted her and stopped. The colt dropped where it stood and lay on its side in deep sleep as the man and mare watched her approach. When she got close, the colt raised its head to look briefly at her, then went back to sleep.

The man watched her without speaking. He looked about her age.

"*Buenos días, Señor.*"

He nodded his head, a small, quick, downward flick of his hat.

"*¿Por favor, tienes agua?* I have come a long way and I am very thirsty."

He sat his horse, looking at her, perhaps contemplating the question, perhaps contemplating the questioner. Then there was another quick flick of the hat.

"*En mi casa.*" He turned his horse and the colt scrambled to its feet. "*¿De dónde vienes?*"

She pointed in the direction of the Uruguay River. "From Argentina. From the other side of the river. I came by boat in the night, and I have been walking all morning."

He stopped his horse and the little colt lay down instantly. The gaucho looked down at her again, at her wrinkled dress and scratched legs, at her muddy shoes and ancient backpack. His face was completely impassive, showing less emotion or curiosity than his mare. Then he nodded, as if concurring with his own thoughts.

"*¿Sabe cómo montar a caballo?*"

"Yes, I know how to ride a horse."

He stepped down and held his hand out for her backpack as she mounted. It had been a long time since she last sat on a traditional gaucho saddle and the filthy sheepskin felt so good to her tired legs she almost sighed in pleasure. The gaucho handed her the reins, braided rawhide greasy with tallow, threw her backpack over his shoulder and started walking without comment. He was even more bowlegged than Hipólito, but he walked with the same small precise steps, rolling from side to side. The little colt scrambled to its feet and followed, alternating between trot and walk.

They traveled in silence for about half an hour before a small adobe cottage came into view, dilapidated and in need of whitewash, a few chickens strutting on the packed earth, an emaciated white hound of indeterminate variety and ancestry asleep under a bare wooden bench. The hound sat up, still partially under the bench, and gave a single perfunctory woof, then scrambled out and upright on all fours, shook vigorously, and stood waving his tail in a languid tempo of greeting. A squat woman who looked as if she might be native Indian came out of the open door, driving a chicken before her.

The gaucho looked up at Pamela. "*¿Tienes hambre?*"

"Yes, thank you, very hungry."

"*Trae algo para comer,*" he called.

There was no fence or demarcation between yard and native brush and pasture, just a gradual diminishing of bare earth, but the horse stopped of its own volition by a tree with bark rubbed smooth just at the height of a horse's head, and Pamela dismounted. The gaucho threw the horse's reins over a branch. He didn't tie them; he simply draped them over, and Pamela knew that if they didn't come out of the house until the next morning the horse would still be standing there. The colt again lay down immediately, exhausted. The woman watched them from the doorway.

"*Dije algo comer,*" the gaucho said again, and the woman turned back into the little house.

They ate outside, the gaucho and his wife sitting on the little bench, Pamela on a three-legged stool he brought out of the house for her. They gave her *maté*, because they had no coffee, and chorizo and black pudding, and an empanada filled with sweet corn and egg to take with her.

She was not the first. Others had come up from the south, a few across the river like her—Pamela wondered if any of those had come from *El Rincón*—some still weak from torture, all fleeing the army, seeking safety.

"But it is not safe here," the gaucho said, "for you or for me if you are found. All this land, all, I don't know how many hundreds of thousands of hectares, belongs to a family with many connections in Montevideo and Buenos Aires both. Police, army, politicians. A lot of money, more than can be imagined. They live in Montevideo, but they have also a hacienda over an hour's ride to the south, a hacienda so grand even the president himself has been to visit. The family's sympathies are with the government."

He spoke as a blind man might speak, one who had never learned the normal range of facial expressions other people use to communicate, using only his mouth, the rest of the face impassive and expressionless.

It was the way, he said, in every country around the world, in the past, today, in the future, always and forever, a few with much, many with very little, and those with much considered death nothing more than a useful tool to help them keep what they had and to take what they wanted. This is neither good nor bad; it is simply the way God has ordained things. For the Charrúas, her ancestors—he tilted his hat toward the woman beside him—it was very bad because they were the many. All they had was the land from this side of the river all the way up into Brazil, land to hunt and fish, but hunting and fishing cannot live side by side with cattle and farming, and so they fought, the Charrúas, against the settlers from Spain and Portugal. And the Charrúas fought so hard and so well the settlers sued for peace and asked all the Charrúas to come to Salsipuedes to talk, to decide how they might divide up the land. But the settlers talked only with their guns, and when the meeting was over, only a handful of Charrúas still lived. So the few killed his wife's ancestors and took the land, but today all Uruguayans call themselves Charrúas when they fight. What is good? What is bad? No man can say. He can say what is good or bad for him, but only God can say what is truly good or truly bad. The meeting at Salsipuedes was bad for the Charrúas, but good for the settlers, yet even then they were not satisfied and they fought against themselves, Blancos against Colorados. Then came the Tupamaros, who wanted the few to share with the many, and there was more bloodshed. Now there is bloodshed again, and when this is over there will be more for some other reason, because a man is never satisfied. He always wants more than he has even when he has more than he needs.

"And you?" Pamela asked. "Are you satisfied? Wouldn't you like at least to be richer than you are?"

For the first time there was a flicker, almost imperceptible, of something in the gaucho's face, perhaps humor, perhaps surprise.

"I am rich. All a man needs is the sky above him and the land below him and a horse to carry him where he wishes. I have these things and more beside. I have a roof over my head. I have clothes on my back. I have food to eat." He patted his belly. "More food than I need. I have other horses in the pasture beyond the trees. I have much more than I need. I am rich. I have always been rich."

He came back from the pasture beyond the trees on a fresh horse and leading a stocky muscular dun. He put another, older saddle on the dun, the sheepskin top piece smelling strongly of horse and mice, and they rode north. Once he veered off the dirt track and took a long way around a wood because, he said, the other way was visible from a road and it would be better—for her, for him, for any others who might follow—if she were not seen.

After several hours they came to a large field with cattle and, on the other side, a hardtop road. He told her where the next town was, but when she asked, he didn't know if it had an airport. He didn't know what town might have an airport. He gave her an old, dented aluminum canteen of water, missing its canvas cover, and told her to keep it upright as much as possible because the top leaked. She told him where the little boat was tied and told him to use it or sell it as he wished. He turned the horses, but before he rode off he swept his hat from his head with a courtly gesture.

"Walk with God. Walk with care."

He trotted back into the brush, leading the dun.

Two days later she crossed the border into Brazil at Rivera on the Uruguay side, Santana do Livramento on the Brazilian side, in a refrigerated milk truck. She sat rigid with fear in the passenger seat, but the border guards on the Uruguay side were hot and bored and barely gave her passport a second glance. A guard on the Brazilian side asked what an Argentinean woman with an English name was doing in a Uruguayan milk truck and she explained she was considering switching from beef cattle to milk cattle and exporting directly into Brazil. He grunted and commented that it was a wise choice as Brazilian beef was every bit as good as Argentinean beef and handed her passport back. Three days after that, a truck carrying rice dropped her a few miles from the airport in Porto Alegre and she used her only credit card to buy a ticket to Rio de Janeiro.

In Rio she used the card again to treat herself to a luxurious stay in an airport hotel where she soaked for an hour in the tub, had her clothes cleaned and pressed, and had wine with her dinner. The next day she left on a direct flight to Dulles Airport, near Washington, DC, in the United States of America. She had a plan.

She had no interest in politics, national or international, but it was well known that Jimmy Carter had enacted arms embargoes against Argentina in an effort to bring an end to human rights violations. She knew Commander-in-Chief Jorge Rafael Videla had been replaced first by General Roberto Eduardo Viola, and ultimately by General Leopoldo Fortunato Galtieri, and that Jimmy Carter had been replaced by Ronald Reagan, but she knew too that America would happily wield its power to protect its reputation as the champion of the oppressed. She would ask America to intervene on her behalf, and before long she would be back in *El Rincón*.

Washington, DC, December, 1981

SHE EXCHANGED HER *PESOS* at Dulles Airport and took a bus into the city. She used her credit card to book a room in the Hilton Hotel on Connecticut Avenue. The hotel was a large crescent-shaped structure, and her map showed it was only a few blocks from the Argentine Embassy and a relatively short walk from the White House, the only seat of government she had heard of in Washington, America's equivalent of *La Casa Rosada*.

The hotel proved to be a bad choice. It was hosting a convention of a group that called themselves 'Shriners,' and the building was packed with drunken men in red fezzes. Three times she opened the door to her room and asked them to quiet down, and each time they apologized profusely and went away, only to be replaced by a new group, louder and more drunk. At last she gave up and tried to doze as best she could with her head sandwiched between two pillows.

In the morning she walked past the Argentine Embassy, pausing to study the building briefly before heading down to the White House. The walk proved longer than she had anticipated, and the city reminded her of a cleaner and more orderly version of Buenos Aires, minus the graffiti and advertising, and minus the giant never-ending tangled nests of electrical and telephone wires overhead, the confused masses of technological and bureaucratic ineptitude that mirrored the political and bureaucratic ineptitude of her homeland.

The White House looked as spotless and pristine as a new bar of soap, the grounds more spacious than she had realized. A large evergreen of some type in a little park across the street was decorated for Christmas, and the air felt almost as chilly as she remembered England to have been nearly sixty years ago. She hadn't thought to pack anything for the northern hemisphere.

She walked around the perimeter of the grounds, past people and families looking through the wrought-iron fence, taking photographs, carrying shopping bags. The main entrance seemed to be on Pennsylvania Avenue and she walked up to one of the immaculate little guard shelters. A young man in a uniform stepped out, straight and trim and hard as a young oak.

"Yes ma'am. Can I help you?"

He had none of the arrogance she associated with the military in Argentina. Instead he radiated professional resolve and courtesy, and she felt encouraged.

"If you please, I know President Reagan is not available to handle such things personally, but perhaps there is an assistant or somebody I might speak to. I have just arrived from Argentina. I had to fly for my life from the army. The military is arresting hundreds of people, perhaps thousands, people they think are resisting them, and I only barely made it out of my house ahead of them. I need help."

"Ma'am, this isn't the place to help you."

"Where do I need to go?"

For a moment he looked at her, his face as impassive and expressionless as the Uruguayan gaucho's. "Hold on." He went back into the little shelter and picked up a phone. He spoke briefly, then either listened for a long time or was put on hold, then spoke again. He finally hung up and came back outside.

"Hold on, ma'am. Someone's coming out to talk to you."

It took about ten minutes and she was starting to get very chilled before another man in uniform walked down the driveway from the White House. He was a little older than the man in the shelter, but clearly cut from the same block of oak.

"Yes, ma'am, how can I help you?"

She repeated herself, adding that she had fled across the river in a boat and made her way first on foot, then on horseback, then by hitching rides on trucks, and finally by plane to here, to America, to Washington, DC.

"Well ma'am, if you want to apply for asylum you have to go to Citizen and Immigration Services, and they're–"

"No. No, I don't want to apply for immigration or anything like that. I want to go home."

"Well, I'm not sure exactly what I can do for you then."

"Who would I talk to about going home? Without being killed, I mean. What branch of your government would be able to influence my government?"

Afterward, she looked back on the moment she spoke those words as an out-of-body experience. It was a phrase she had heard and read, but never given any thought to before, but suddenly, as she spoke, she seemed to stand outside and slightly above herself, watching and listening to herself, an elderly woman inappropriately dressed on the sidewalk outside the most famous building in the world, mouthing preadolescent inanities as if she were the center of the universe, and for the first time she realized how much bigger America was than Argentina, geographically, politically, economically, in every way, how insignificant she was in the face of all that wealth and power and influence, and how foolish she was to have even wasted the energy to walk all the way down here to whine like a child to these two polite impassive men. For the first time since she had fled the library at *El Rincón*, half dragged by Hipólito, the magnitude of her situation hit her along with the insignificance of that magnitude compared to the rest of the world. She felt tears come into her eyes, tears of despair, of self-pity, and above all tears of embarrassment for being so foolish and naïve. She turned her head away.

"The only thing I can suggest, ma'am, is that you talk to someone at the State Department. They have someone who deals with South America and maybe they can give you some advice."

"Where is the State Department?"

"It's actually called the Department of State and it's on C Street."

He gave her directions, taking a step closer to her and pointing along Pennsylvania Avenue, and she had to resist the impulse to rest her head on his chest.

The Department of State had none of the elegance or sense of history of the White House or so much of Washington. Instead, it reminded Pamela of photographs she had seen of grey bureaucratic administration buildings in Communist Russia, impersonal, monolithic, inhuman. The security guard matched the building, as impassive as the men at the White House, but less forthcoming. There was no one there who could help her and he had no idea where she might go to get help. Finally, she played the only card she could think of and drew herself up to her full height.

"You have a section devoted to South American affairs—"

"There is no section of South American affairs. There is a Bureau of Inter-American Affairs, and that's it."

"Very well. You tell the head of your Bureau of Inter-American Affairs that Pamela Trevelyan wishes to speak to him, that my family and I are long-time friends of our current president, General Leopoldo Galtieri, and that neither my family nor President Galtieri will be pleased if the United States of America refuses to help a citizen of Argentina, an allied country whose strategic importance to the United States is well known to your head of the Bureau of Inter-American Affairs, even if it is not to you."

She lingered slightly on the final 'you,' filling it with the dismissive contempt of an employer for an inept and ill-mannered servant. There was not a syllable of truth to any of her story, but she knew this very minor bureaucratic lump in front of her wouldn't know that.

"Furthermore, you tell your head of–"

"Alright, Ma'am! I'm going to have to ask you to sit down and be quiet. I'll call someone."

Ten minutes later a secretary escorted her past the guards, up an elevator, down an overheated corridor, and into an overheated office where she was asked to sit and wait. Twenty minutes later the phone rang and after a brief conversation the secretary escorted her into an even hotter and stuffier waiting room and once more asked her to sit and wait. More time passed. She studied a large framed photograph of a smiling President Reagan looking neither particularly presidential nor even like a former movie star, but like a typical amiable, good-humored, successful American businessman, the kind of man who might be an enjoyable seat companion on a long flight.

A plump man came in who looked as if he had been manufactured to match the building, grey, mass produced, built for standing in or dealing with long lines of anonymous people whose problems were of no interest or concern to him.

"Are you the head of the Bureau of Inter-American Affairs?"

"No. The Assistant Secretary of State for Inter-American Affairs is Mr. Enders, but he is not here at the moment. I am the Under Assistant Secretary of State for Inter-American Affairs, and I am acting on Secretary Enders' behalf. What may I do for you?"

She told her story again, emphasizing Jimmy Carter's attempt to restore human rights by pressuring the Argentine government with an arms embargo, and reiterating her desire to go home.

He listened quietly and when she was finished he sat looking at her as if expecting something more.

At last he took a deep breath and let it out in a carefully moderated expression of exasperation. "I assume you are aware that Ronald Reagan is the current President of the United States?"

"Yes, of course."

"So whatever policies that might have been put in place by President Reagan's Democratic predecessor would only be left in place if President Reagan deemed them expedient and necessary. You understand that?" He spoke as if she were an intelligent but willful child.

"Yes."

"Good. Then let me explain to you that, in general, the attitudes and goals of the current administration are very different than those of the previous administration. Let me also explain that in any case it is not the policy of the United States to interfere or intervene with a foreign sovereign government on behalf of any single citizen of that government. If you wished to apply for political asylum you would have to go through the appropriate channels, but as you have stated that it is your desire to return to your home, there is absolutely nothing the United States government can or will do for you."

"That's it?"

"That's it."

"Do you—I mean you personally—have any suggestions, anything you can think of that I might try?"

"No. Speaking for the Department of State in general, I would suggest you speak to representatives of your government."

"You mean talk to the Ambassador?"

"To somebody at the Argentine embassy, yes." He gave the impression of using all his willpower not to call out, "Next!"

She waited for almost an hour in the front hall of the Argentine embassy before a secretary came out and asked if she could take Pamela's passport to the Ambassador. It was only as the secretary closed a heavy wooden door behind her that Pamela had a moment of doubt, of suspicion, but by then it was too late.

Two hours passed. The clock was an inexpensive industrial-looking thing, out of place in the formality of the hall, and she spent the time imaging the conversations taking place between the Ambassador and someone—possibly even General Galtieri—in *La Casa Rosada*, and what kind of a problem she presented to them, and what kind of a solution they would come up with.

Finally, a younger and more handsome version of the American Under Assistant Secretary of State for Inter-American Affairs came out into the hall. He stood in front of her and folded manicured hands with polished nails over a plump little belly in an attitude that conveyed he had far more important things to attend to.

"Mrs. Trevelyan–"

"Usted puede hablar en español si lo desea."

"No, Mrs. Trevelyan, I choose to speak in English. You have caused the government of Argentina great distress. You are a left-wing subversive and you have provided aid to other left-wing subversives. These are things that will not be tolerated. If you wish to go back to Argentina, you will go back as a prisoner and an enemy of the government."

"I've never heard such rubbish in all my life. I am–"

"Mrs. Trevelyan! There are papers out for your immediate arrest in Argentina. You are an enemy of the state and as long as you remain out of the country the government has no interest in your affairs or your concerns. No interest whatsoever. You do not exist. If you wish to return to Argentina, please let me know and I will make arrangements for the army to take you into custody as you step off the plane. Otherwise…" He made a dismissive gesture with the tips of his manicured fingers and turned to go.

"Wait. Give me my passport."

"Your passport has been confiscated, Mrs. Trevelyan."

"You can't do that!"

He simply looked at her and said nothing.

"You can't do that. This is America and I–"

"You are a very ignorant woman, Mrs. Trevelyan. This is not America. Under international law an embassy is the sovereign property of the government it represents. In this building you are on Argentine property, and the only reason you have not been arrested is because you are too insignificant for us to take any interest in you. Get out, or I will have you arrested."

He turned and walked back through the heavy wooden door without waiting to see what she might do.

Washington, DC, December, 1981

IN HER ROOM IN THE CRESCENT-SHAPED Hilton hotel she sat on the bed. Inside it was quiet now, the drunken Shriners either having checked out or still sleeping it off. She could hear traffic on Connecticut Avenue, the muted cacophony of car engines, sporadic horns, a siren so different from the sirens of Buenos Aires she couldn't tell if it was police or ambulance or fire truck, but with the same imperious urgency, the occasional deep rumble of a diesel, the squeal of brakes, all of it blending together to make a distant and meaningless background noise, the squabbling of urban parakeets heard through closed windows.

The Argentinean official, whose name and title she didn't even know, had used the word 'insignificant' as if he had instinctively known how she was feeling. At a party she had once heard someone—a doctor, a psychiatrist, someone in the medical profession—say there is always an unspoken, intuitive relationship between the criminal and his victim, the bully and the bullied, the predator and his prey, that the person who must dominate will always seek out and find the person who will allow themselves to be dominated, and that the dominated will seek equally for someone to dominate them. She had dismissed it then as intellectual strutting, but now...

She had been one thing. Now she was something else, something insignificant.

She had thought, dimly, abstractly, of her world—*El Rincón*, the ridiculous house, the paintings and furniture and silver, the horses and cattle, the greater world of beloved friends and servants—as enduring in a state of stasis, waiting for her return. Now for the first time she began to see return as something that might never happen and she tried to imagine that world without her. Where were Hipólito and his mother, Maria? Where were the other gauchos? Where was Risada? Were her things still there in the house? Where did the red chalk Edward Robert Hughes portrait of her mother as a young bride now hang? She should have prepared, taken steps, hidden things and people, sent them somewhere, done... what? Something, anything.

She began to sob with the deep, gasping despair of absolute hopelessness, irrevocable loss, the finality of death.

She woke with a plan. She had heard through the social grapevine that a second cousin of Ian's had been made consul general in Los Angeles. She had never met him, but he had written a kind and elegant condolence letter from Australia after Ian's death. He was young enough to have been Ian's son, but his letter captured the wit and charm of the dead man well enough to make her smile, enough to make her remember him now. She would fly to Los Angeles and beg for help.

With the plan came hope, and with hope came hunger. She ordered room service and watched the news as she ate. The English was perfectly understandable, but she was intrigued by the differences, the strange pronunciation of some of the words, the peculiar structure of some of their sentences, and the different names for some things. Why did the news reader pronounce "schedule" as if it were spelled with a "k?" Why did a congressman cut off an interview saying, "Excuse me, I got a meeting with the Vice President," without the "have?" Soviet missiles were pronounced like whistles. How could rams from Los Angeles have mauled lions from Detroit and what did that mean? A fanny pack sounded vulgar to her ear.

She debated going out to buy some clothes, but decided against it. The shops would probably be closed by this time, and besides, she had heard it was always warm and sunny in Los Angeles no matter what the season. Better to wait and buy what she needed out there.

She sat on the foot of the bed and jumped from channel to channel. She had no television at *El Rincón* and the little she had seen in Argentina was very different from this frenetic, high octane, action driven bouillabaisse of youth and beauty. There seemed to be something for everyone: lugubrious soap operas; wacky comedy shows, where unseen people laughed hysterically after every second line; action shows with fistfights and car chases and guns; a science show about the formation of islands; a panel of men discussing the effect of President Reagan's policies on the cost of oil; a game show where people were expected to answer ridiculous questions. America, as portrayed on its television, seemed to be a world unto itself, a place where everything worked and nothing was ever too terribly wrong, nothing that couldn't be solved with a laugh and a wink and a moment's casual conversation. It was not a place where an emaciated girl would huddle in a horse stall recounting horrors in a weary monotone.

She got up early, determined to be at Dulles Airport as soon as possible, but her plans began to unravel when she went downstairs to check out.

"I'm sorry. There's a problem with your card."

The checkout girl was black and very pretty, her hair braided into hundreds of tight strings that were pulled tightly back into a heavy hawser cable. She had a slight accent, a sort of sing-song, as if she had learned English very well in a land where it was not the native tongue.

"What do you mean? What kind of problem?"

"It says here your card has been canceled."

"That's nonsense. It's my account. I haven't canceled anything."

"Well, I'll try it again. Sometimes things get mixed up."

The girl did something with her hands below the counter and gave Pamela a little smile as they waited. After several moments she frowned at her little machine.

"No, it says your account has been closed."

Pamela stared at the girl. She felt cold, cold with fear, cold with certainty.

"Would you like to speak to the manager?" The girl's tone was carefully modulated between helpful and non-committal.

"No." It came out as a croak and she had to clear her throat. "No, thank you. Just tell me how much I owe you."

The girl told her, and Pamela pulled out her American dollars, so new and unfamiliar to her. She counted out the amount slowly and carefully, and then, as the girl's fingers recounted them swiftly and nimbly, Pamela counted what she had left. It was very little. Other people were trickling into the lobby, waiting to check out. Someone was standing behind her with a large suitcase.

"Do you need anything else?" The girl's tone was still carefully and politely modulated, only now there was slightly less emphasis on the helpful.

"No. Thank you."

She went over to the sitting area. The chairs were designed to discourage lingering, stiff and uncomfortable, covered with fabric that felt bulletproof. She sat in the inappropriate summer clothes grabbed hastily in the dark, with her ancient canvas backpack, and watched well-dressed men and women in tailored suits, wearing or carrying raincoats and overcoats, with suitcases and garment bags, all with a sense of purpose and urgency, places to go, things to do and accomplish, appointments to keep, timetables to follow, homes and lives to return to, people waiting for them, families expecting them.

She counted her money again. It was still very little, far too little to buy a plane ticket to Los Angeles. In desperation she counted it a third time.

When there was a break in the stream of checkouts, Pamela went back to the counter. The girl looked at her with a neutral expression poised to refuse any request.

"What is the cheapest way to get to Los Angeles?"

The bus station had a stylized image of a greyhound above the word itself, and the waiting area had the stale smell of cigarettes and diesel fumes, too many people and too much poverty. She sat with her ticket in her hand and her backpack on her lap. She had almost five hours to wait, but she had neither the energy nor the courage to go anywhere. It had been a long walk from the Hilton and her feet and knees throbbed, and the people she had passed as she neared the station scared her. She had seen very few black people in her life, and the ones on the streets in this dirty, littered neighborhood were loud and boisterous and had a youthful air of unpredictability and violence. There were only two other white people in the waiting area, a couple about her age, the man unshaven, both unclean and smelling strongly of whiskey, so she sat next to a young black soldier. She had no way of judging his rank from his uniform, but he sat very straight and looked disciplined and competent and she took comfort from his presence. When he left, still several hours before her bus departed, she became nervous and watchful, but no one bothered her.

Afterward, she remembered the trip as something between a nightmare and a dream: endless hours of discomfort, uneasy and unsuccessful attempts to sleep as the bus rumbled through the dark; long waits to discharge or take on passengers or change buses in stations that all looked and smelled identical, then on again, out past the diminishing lights of unknown towns and cities, sitting cramped and upright, trying to make a kind of pillow out of her backpack, never fully resting.

Against that were the daylight hours driving through landscapes very different from anything she had seen before, fields lying fallow under leaden skies, framed by endless woods, larger fields covered with snow and sunlight so bright it hurt her eyes; the shocking cold when they disembarked on a sunny afternoon in some city, cold so intense it was palpable, something that could be broken off in chunks and saved for future use; the vastness of the visible land and the way it changed so gradually over such great distances; long stretches completely free of any sign of human influence; mountains almost as high and rugged as the Andes; land drier than she had thought possible, until at last, after two days and three nights, or perhaps three days and two nights she got out for the last time, her teeth covered with moss, her eyes packed with sand, her skin and scalp oily, stretching and yawning in the embracing warmth of an almost Argentinean sun, a sun that gave her hope.

She got the address for the Consulate out of the telephone directory and then waited in the ticket line. The man behind the counter was probably forty years younger than she, but he looked weary beyond all reckoning, not sleepy or tired, but world weary, as if the years of selling tickets to an endless current of the poor had abraded all life and energy or even interest from him.

"Where to?"

"I need directions." She gave him the address on Wilshire Boulevard.

"That's east. Go up Seventh to Wilshire. Head east." He sighed heavily, as if that had taken more out of him than he had to spare.

"How far is it?"

"I don't know."

"Is there a bus or a trolley I can take?"

"Trolley?

"Streetcar."

"There's no streetcar. Might be a bus, but I don't know."

"Where could I get a bus?"

"I don't know."

"How much would it cost?"

"I don't know."

"Do you know how long will it take to walk?"

For the first time there was a faint flicker of life. "That's a long way, lady. Two hours, probably."

It took her almost three hours. She didn't walk far enough at the outset to find Wilshire, and the first person she asked for directions sent her the wrong way. Her feet and knees started protesting long before she got there, and she longed to hail a taxi, but she had less than seventeen dollars left. If the Consul was unable or unwilling or afraid to help her…

She expected something like the embassy in Washington, an elegant private building. Instead, it was a suite of offices in an anonymous beige and grey high-rise, a building so unremarkable it might equally have housed beige and grey CPAs or beige and grey CIA agents. It was distinguished only by being the largest building on the block, and by having ficus trees planted in front instead of palms.

A very fashionably dressed young woman behind a counter was speaking Spanish on the phone.

"*Martes.*" She smiled cheerfully at Pamela and held up one finger. "*No, martes.*" A pause. "*Sí.*" And then, incongruously, "*Ciao.*"

She hung up, still smiling at Pamela.

"How can I help you?"

"My name is Pamela Trevelyan. I'd like to see St. John Guzman. He's a cousin of my late husband…" She trailed off. Her first thought was that her name had been put on a list, Argentina's Most Wanted, People to Beware Of, Enemies of the State, because the fashionable young woman's mouth had opened into a perfect 'O.' One hand came up to her breast, then moved up to cover the open mouth.

For a moment they simply looked at each other, and knowing already her cause was hopeless without even knowing why, she felt a wave of anger and resentment, seeing herself through the eyes of this elegant and clean young woman: old, rumpled, unwashed, brittle white hair unbrushed, slightly stooped, her wrinkled skin blotched with liver spots and sun damage, joints swollen with arthritis, clutching an ancient canvas backpack, and she thought, "I was once as young and pretty as you and no one looked at me with pity or disdain simply because of my years."

But when the young woman spoke she said, "I'm sorry, Mr. Guzman had a heart attack."

"A heart attack?"

"Yes. I'm sorry."

"Where is he?"

"His body was sent back to Buenos Aires, oh, almost three weeks ago."

"His body?" She was tired and disoriented and having trouble absorbing the information.

"Yes. I'm sorry," she said again. "We had a memorial service for him here the Saturday before last. No. Three Saturdays ago."

There were brochures on the counter, one with a photograph of the Jesuit Block and its Church of the *Compañia de Jesús* in Córdoba, another with yachts in the harbor of Buenos Aires. There was a large color photograph of General Galtieri on the wall. She passed her hand over her eyes.

"Would you like to sit down?" The young woman stood up. "Are you alright?"

"Who is the consul now?"

"Oh, he hasn't arrived yet. Would you like to speak to someone else, someone from Culture, or Economy and Trade?" She glanced at her watch. "I think Mr. Gonzales is still here."

She thought of the plump and manicured man in the Embassy who had dismissed her as insignificant; she remembered Colonel Francisco Pieres keeping his back to her in fear as he stomped divots on the polo field; the lights of the trucks as they came down the allée. "¡*Dése prisa, Señora! ¡Por Dios!*"

"No. No, thank you."

She spent her first night as a homeless person in someone's back yard. There was a residential neighborhood just north of the consulate, clean streets of well-maintained houses, walled gardens, swimming pools, an air of comfortable prosperity. She bought a bag of nuts in a convenience store—sixteen dollars left—and ate them as she walked through the darkening streets. Most of the homes were brightly lit with life inside and Christmas decorations outside, but a house on a corner lot appeared to be vacant. She kept walking, returning again and again in the dark to that street, and finally, when no lights came on, she climbed over a wrought iron gate. In desperation she peed behind some bushes in a corner where the wall met the driveway and quickly washed her face and armpits in the swimming pool and drank out of a hose. The temperature was dropping rapidly, but the side of the garage faced west and retained a slight reminder of the day's warmth so she lay down in the flower bed against the wall and despite the cold, despite her fear and despair and hunger, fell instantly asleep.

A sound woke her. She opened her eyes, but she was so disoriented that she made no effort to move. Lights came on along a brick path by the pool, and a door from the garage, not ten feet from her head, opened. A man and woman walked to the house, arguing, the woman hissing quiet accusations, the man contemptuously dismissive, something to do with his or someone else's behavior at a party.

Lights in the house went on, and the lights outside went off. For awhile she lay awake on her side, shivering, backpack under her head, watching the progression of the argument from room to room and sometimes back again, silhouettes against windows, shadows against blinds, lights on, lights off, until she fell asleep once more.

The next time she woke she thought it was raining. It was the pale grey before dawn and an automatic sprinkler system had come on. She grabbed her pack and fled back out into the city.

She began to learn the ways of the city and life on the streets. It was like learning from a horse, watching subtle changes in body language and interaction to determine the character and needs of a mute but dangerously powerful organism. She tried to find work, asking to be allowed to wait on tables or wash dishes in restaurants, mop floors, scrub toilets, anything, but even after making herself as clean and presentable as possible she still had the aura, perhaps a smell, of the homeless, the desperate, or perhaps no one needed or wanted a seventy-two year old woman. The closest she got was at a bookstore, where her English accent and obvious education almost landed her a chance to fill out an application, but when the manager realized she had no green card, no passport, no social security number, no driver's license, no American identification of any kind, he took the papers back almost in fear, as if a woman without a country might possibly be contagious.

Her tiny store of cash dwindled.

She observed other homeless ones from a distance and discovered which trash cans were most likely to have edible food. She was kicked awake in certain kinds of doorways, but had to share or flee from others. She noticed immediately how people—and not just the homeless—looked at her wedding ring and she took it off, with difficulty, for the first time since Ian had slipped it on half a century ago— the feel of his hand, his clean taut freshly shaved cheek, the smell of his soap mingling with the smell of the church, her mother smiling though tears—hiding it in a pocket of her backpack. She learned how to carry herself and behave in fast food places so that she could use a bathroom without attracting attention and being turned away.

She was able to get fifty dollars for her watch from a customer in a pawn shop, a watch Ian had paid over a thousand for almost forty years ago. The pawn store owner refused to buy it because she had no identification, but the customer followed her out and even though she knew she was being robbed she was grateful and almost dizzy with the sense of wealth. She even contemplated buying some food, but knew that would be unwise and frivolous.

Almost two weeks into her new life, a filthy and profane woman who called herself Eddie shared an entry with her one night, and when they were chased off by a security guard, Eddie told her of a place on the edges of a park, at the foot of the hills where the word Hollywood was spelled out in giant white letters, a place where the homeless were left more or less in peace to sleep under bushes that grew in the lee of a highway overpass. She volunteered to show Pamela the spot, but less than halfway there she had some sort of fit and wandered off raging at someone who wasn't there, causing people on the street to swerve away and around her like water around a rock. A police car stopped, and Pamela could see the officer watching and talking on his radio. She turned away and walked on.

She found the place easily enough—the lessons and instincts of the disenfranchised and unnoticed are quickly learned—a settlement of flattened pieces of cardboard and miscellaneous rubbish on earth worn bare and hard beneath the bushes, smelling strongly of urine. The cement wall of the overpass was covered in a calligraphic mosaic of graffiti, most of it the hastily sprayed-on symbols of gang turf, but at one end someone had artfully painted an elaborate cartoon of three creatures with giant feet and giant hands and floppy hats walking and smiling, and it was only after looking at it, admiring it, that she realized it spelled out the words, Made You Look, Didn't I?

She had recovered the tail end of a cappuccino. She had learned to hang around take-out food places, changing streets and neighborhoods to avoid drawing the attention of the police. She would wait and then follow the obviously affluent who invariably bought more than they could eat or drink, much as she had always left food on her plate at *El Rincón* without ever considering what happened to it. She had seen a man, well-dressed, corpulent, attaché case in one hand, the cardboard cup in the other, and she had followed him and pounced on the garbage can as soon as he dropped the cup.

Now she sat with her back against the spray-painted art and sipped the half-full cup, reveling in the once familiar taste of good beans darkly roasted. She knew she had to think about work, about survival, about some kind of future, but the sun was almost down and the stored warmth of the cement felt good, and for a few moments she allowed herself the luxury of neither worrying nor even thinking. In the distance, over the background drone of the city, she could hear a carillon playing "Oh, Silent Night," and realized it was Christmas Eve.

"They're coming, you know."

She opened her eyes. A young man with a beard was standing a few feet away. He wasn't looking at her and she turned her head to see whom he might be speaking to, but there was no one else there. She had no memory of falling asleep. Judging by the light, the cappuccino still lukewarm in her hand, she hadn't, yet she hadn't heard him approach.

"They're coming," he said again.

"Who's coming?"

"Just four more years. A little more. 1986. They'll come, and I'm going with them."

He was cleaner and better dressed and better spoken than anyone she expected to see in a homeless encampment, than any of the homeless she had encountered, his shoes polished, a new windbreaker. He held an orange in one hand and the sight of it brought a literal rush of saliva in her mouth.

"Who?"

"They're coming, and the dead will go with them. Not all the dead. Just those of us who understand. And we're not really dead, of course." For the first time he looked directly at her. "There's salvation and music and peace. You don't need money. You don't need food or clothes or a house or parents. You don't need anything. You're always happy. It's beautiful. It's always peaceful. It *is* peace." His eyes shone. "See, that's what people don't understand. You've read the Bible. You know about Heaven and Hell, right? Well, this is Hell. Where we are now? On this planet? In this life? In this temporal plane? This is Hell. Look around you. Look at the pain and suffering. Look at the hunger and injustice. Look at all the wars and famines and diseases. Look at all the pollution and the filth. Look at the corruption everywhere, the imbalance between rich and poor." He waved his hand down the slope toward the city. "Look at it all. This is Hell. You see that, don't you? It's Hell. If you've been here, it means you've served your sentence, you're free to go. All you have to do is take that step, that one little step, and you'll be free."

As if moved by his own suggestion he took one little step toward her. She drew her legs up and put the cappuccino down by her side.

"You know the great thing, the really great thing? Well, it's just one of the great things. All this pollution and noise, and all these things we build to keep warm, to go places, to bring us back from places we've gone to, houses and cars and jets, the bombs and missiles we make to kill the people we don't like, all of that stuff, that negative stuff, it doesn't exist there. You don't need it there."

She looked left and right as casually as she could. It was starting to get dark.

"Don't worry. There's no one else here. I wouldn't tell you all this if there were anyone else."

She looked back up at him.

"And do you know how they do it? They tap into us. That's how they do it. Scientists have done these studies that show, that prove, we only use ten percent of our brains. Who is using the other ninety percent? They are! That's why they're able to do all the stuff we can't. That's why they're able to live in Heaven. I can tell, I can feel it when they're using me, my brain. And the spaceship that is going to take us, you know how they fuel that? They use our energy." The words were coming out faster. "I don't mean gasoline or coal or anything like that. I'm talking about opposites, all the opposites that are here in this plane, on this planet that we call Earth but is really Hell. All those opposites, up and down, back and forth, black and white, good and evil, rich and poor, all those opposites—the friction, the conflict between them—that creates energy and they tap into it and they use it, just like they use the ninety percent of our brains that we don't use, and they take all that energy and do whatever they need to with it. It's clean. It doesn't pollute. It's pure. And it's never-ending."

He reached under the windbreaker and pulled out a knife, a survival type of thing with a black blade and a serrated saw edge on the back, and she knew. She knew absolutely. It was the serrated edge that terrified her and she wondered if it would help to scream in this place that was in the center of the city, yet isolated from it.

He drew the blade slowly and carefully over the orange, completely around in one direction, then completely around the other way, across the original cut, dividing the peel into four parts.

It was his diction and precise use of language that gave her the idea to keep him talking and she said the first thing that popped into her head.

"You haven't told me who."

He looked at her, orange in one hand, dripping slightly, knife in the other. "Who?"

"You said they were coming, that they can do all these things. Who are they?"

"The Old Ones. The ones that came before." He moved the orange slightly in one direction, then the knife in the other, as if to indicate the vastness of the world beyond the bushes, beyond the city, beyond borders and oceans. "Think of all the people who are on this planet now. What is it? Four billion, five billion? Now think of all the people that have been on this planet since the very beginning. It's a staggering number to think of, isn't it? But now consider this: this planet that we know, where we are now, it's only one of countless billions of planets in this universe, and this universe is only one of countless billions of universes. And that's only one physical plane. This orange is made up of countless billions of atoms, and each of those atoms is an entire universe, just like ours, just as full of life and mystery and diversity as ours, with people as numerous and varied as ours. In fact, cutting this peel, I have killed countless trillions of people. I have just wiped out entire galaxies. When I eat this orange, it will be the end of countless minuscule worlds and universes." He giggled. "I am the god of this orange. But now let's go the other way. You and I, this world, this universe that we inhabit, is only an atom in an orange held in the hand of someone who is himself merely an atom in a vaster plane. And it goes on from there, on and on and on, never-ending. Do you see?"

The pitch of his voice had risen and he was breathing heavily, gesturing more with knife and orange both.

"And that's just the physical plane, up and down, in and out, greater and larger, all the opposites we talked about. Now consider the temporal planes, all the universes of all the different sizes that exist where we exist in time are completely different from all the universes that exist just a second behind us, and those are different from the ones that exist just a second ahead of us. Now think of all eternity, backwards and forwards. The different planes—"

He looked off to the side and, as suddenly as he had appeared, he turned and walked away.

A giant black man with matted dreadlocks was making his way into the bushes. He wore a filthy trench coat and carried a push broom over his shoulder and plastic grocery bags in his other hand.

Her first thought was to leave and find some other place, but the black man never looked at her or acknowledged her, and her fear had left her drained and exhausted. And there was no other place to go.

She woke with a hand clamped over her mouth. For an instant she was confused and thought it was Hipólito waking her, warning her. Then she realized it must be the giant black man and terror went through her in a nauseous wave, and she felt another hand fumbling at her belt. She began to struggle and realized a third hand, someone else, was holding her arms above her head.

"Stay still, bitch."

And she knew from the voice it wasn't the giant. She could see a smaller man's silhouette above her.

The hand at her waist got her belt undone and opened the front of her slacks and she tried to thrash harder, but whoever was pulling her slacks down was straddling her. He pulled the slacks first on one side, then the other, and then he lifted himself slightly to pull her pants down around her buttocks and as he did so the edge of his hand went into her mouth.

She bit down with all her strength, feeling a bone between her teeth.

There was a scream of rage and pain. "You fucking cunt," and he slapped at the side of her head, but she held on. "Goddamn you, fuck," and this time he punched her on the forehead hard enough to make fireworks go off. He pulled his hand free.

"You fucking little—"

He appeared to levitate above her, and in her dazed state she thought he might have gotten up to jump on her and she tried to tense her body against the impact, but instead he vanished and there was a yell, a noise, a grunt of pain. Whoever held her arms let go and said, "No," but whatever he said no to happened because there was a sound she realized must be a bone breaking followed by a scream of pain.

She tried to roll over and pull up her pants and run all at once, but she collided with someone. She stumbled and started to fall but the person she collided with caught her.

"Easy now. Easy." As if she were a horse. And she realized from the voice, the size of the shape in front of her, it was the black man. She recoiled in fear, and this time she did fall down, sitting down hard, gasping, choking, starting to sob.

The huge shape in front of her squatted down. "You okay? They hurt you bad?"

She couldn't speak.

"This ain't no place for no white lady be sleeping here. You better come on over by me case those two boys try and come on back."

He helped her up—picked her up, really—and guided her away. She couldn't stop crying, sobbing with the helpless uncontrolled despair of a child, staggering and stumbling in the dark, twice nearly falling, held up only by the strength of this terrible, terrifying unknown man beside her.

At some indiscernible spot in the dark he eased her down and she heard the rustling of plastic.

"You hungry?"

He placed a Styrofoam container in her hands and she sat holding it, still crying, aware even as she wept, even through her congested nose and hiccups, that whatever was in the box smelled better than any food she had eaten since the hotel in Washington, smells of ginger and garlic and other spices she couldn't identify, and as her sobs subsided into childlike gasps and coughing, her attention became more and more focused on the food. Then they heard a groan from where she had been sleeping.

"My pack! They're still there! I left my bag."

The giant black moved away, vanishing in the dark as she sat, the food in her hands forgotten, listening to the rustling of the bushes, yells and curses, another scream of pain, more curses diminishing in the dark, and the rustling of bushes again. Something brushed her shoulder and she grabbed her pack.

"They gone."

They sat in the dark, she waiting for her breathing to return to normal, her chest and stomach sore from weeping, alternately reveling in the smells from the Styrofoam box, and cautiously exploring the growing knot on her forehead with her fingertips, and he... What was he doing in the dark? The only light in this corner of the park was the dim strobe-like reflected glow from cars and trucks passing above them, but that barely penetrated the density of shadows that were more substantial than the trees and bushes that cast them. She was aware of his presence, his bulk, could tell he was sitting, but what was he looking at, what was he thinking, what might he do next?

At last she was calm enough to eat, putting the cold noodles and bits of shrimp and broccoli in her mouth with her fingers, eating it all, sucking on her fingers, licking the bottom of the box, probing her tongue into each corner with lascivious pleasure, yawning deeply even before she put the container down.

"Thank you. Thank you so much. That was delicious. It was the best food I've had in, oh, weeks. It was so good. What was it?"

There was a long pause. "Thai."

"Thai food? I don't think I've ever had Thai food before. It was heavenly. Where did you get it?"

No answer.

"Thank you also for… for saving me. Thank you."

No response.

"I'm Pamela. What's your name?"

Nothing.

They sat in the dark. She had no idea what he might do, but fatigue was overwhelming her as if she had been drugged, and when she finally nearly toppled over she gave up the struggle and lay down with her pack under her head and slept more deeply and completely than she had in a long time. Once she partially woke and was aware he was doing something, something to her, but she was too tired even to be scared and whatever he did hadn't hurt her, and she fell back asleep before she could even make herself wake up enough to find out what was happening.

She woke in the morning with what Ian had called, quoting one of his favorite poets, the rough male kiss of wool about her face. The black man had put a piece of what had once been a blanket over her. It had been burned badly, about a third of it missing, and it smelled strongly of him, but she lay quietly, luxuriating in unaccustomed warmth.

Over time, through the days and nights of the next week, she learned his name was Tony, but not from him. He had specific routines and places, where people seemed to know him and like him. Once even a white police officer thrust his arm out the window of his car and waved, calling him by name.

She also learned he wouldn't answer any questions about himself, only about neutral things: where to get a drink of water, where to find a bathroom. He maintained a constant unending conversation with someone, a soft susurration into the past, question and response and memory. Occasionally he would become agitated, but it took the form of grief, not violence or even anger, and once as they walked down Vine Street, he wept softly and quietly as if his heart would break, and she took his arm, half afraid of how he might react. But he did nothing. He neither stopped walking nor crying. He didn't even acknowledge her touch, but he didn't pull away either, and they walked arm in arm for several blocks until his normal quiet monologue resumed.

One late afternoon, walking in an alley behind small businesses and restaurants, they passed a bistro with its door propped open and she heard a tango she knew well, not the arrangement or voice she knew, something softer and gentler, but unmistakably *La Cumparsita*.

"Tony!"

He stopped, talking and walking both, and she took the broom out of his hand and put his arm around her waist and began to dance. It took a few moments for her to overcome his surprise and for him to pick up on her movements, but he was quick and graceful, and they danced amid the smells of food and garbage, the plastic bags in his hand swinging with their movements, past dumpsters and broken bottles, past a parked delivery van and an Hispanic man dressed in white chef's clothes in the doorway of the bistro who stopped and stared and when the music ended he threw his arms in the air and called, "*¡Hermosa! ¡Encantador!*"

Then it was over. Tony picked up his broom and they walked on, he talking softly again to himself or someone else, she breathless with dancing and delight and her own memories.

Los Angeles, 1982

SHE SAT IN THE SUN on the asphalt next to his collection of plastic bags, her back against the cinderblock wall of whatever the next building was—she hadn't even cared enough to notice—and watched Tony sweeping the sidewalk on the two sides of a Shell gas station on the corner of Vine and Santa Monica in Hollywood, California, the United States of America, a country she and Ian had always intended to visit.

The city was not at all what she had expected. After more than two months she had learned it wasn't even a single city. It was a collection of unattractive cities packed together on a plain between an ocean she knew must be somewhere out there to the west and mountains she could barely see for the brown haze that hung in the air. There was no architectural coherence. There were very few trees, mostly unhealthy looking palms that provided no shade. There was a constant guttural roaring of car engines, so many of them that it became a loud but meaningless background noise, like living next to the cataract of some polluted river. The brown air had a metallic smell that reminded her of the taste of something from childhood that hovered just outside the reach of her memory. There was nothing she could see, no building, no matter where she looked, that had any visual appeal, nothing to inspire or delight the eye.

There weren't many pedestrians—the city seemed to move exclusively by car—but the ones that did walk by gave Tony a wide berth. It was a curious dynamic. He was clearly lost in his own world, talking softly and constantly to himself, not angrily, never ranting, but frequently stopping his sweeping to use his hands, gesturing forcefully in the air as if he might be giving directions, or demonstrating how to use some tool or piece of machinery. Despite their strength and vigor, there was something curiously Italianate about those movements in the air, so that a giant black man with matted dreadlocks in a filthy trench coat reminded her of the young men, slim and graceful and elegant as the shotguns they carried, who used to come for weekend shooting parties at *El Rincón*, laughing by the fireplace in the library, using their hands to illustrate a political theory, a difficult shot made that afternoon, a quotation from Ovid, the curve of a girl's waist or a building's façade, abstractions and specifics all expressed by hands moving through the air, as now Tony used his hands to express something that troubled him to whoever it was he talked to. He was engrossed in his conversation, but also aware of the pedestrians, sweeping one side of the sidewalk or the other, always giving plenty of room to the people who veered equally away from him. And the more dangerous the pedestrians, the more afraid they seemed to be of him, so that ugly knots of teenaged boys—black or white or Hispanic, with boisterous voices and tattoos and contemptuous sneers, spreading across the sidewalk, demanding space as their inalienable and exclusive right—became suddenly quiet, walking single file, eyes rolling warily or looking sullenly at the ground as they increased their pace in wide arcs around him.

She sat on the ground in the sun and watched him, this man who had saved and helped her, this man to whom she now felt bound by her need for protection, by her ignorance of this city and this country and the rules and laws and customs of both, by her own fear, by her inability to survive. She sat on the ground in the parking lot of a gas station in an ugly city in an unfamiliar land and the magnitude of her situation suddenly swept over her, leaving her breathless and somehow hollow. She wasn't just homeless. She was more than homeless, far more than Tony or the others sleeping in the bushes on the edges of Griffith Park, because she had no nationality. She needed a new word for her condition. She had ceased to exist. She had nothing, who had once presided over a world of fertile land and countless numbers of cattle, of polo ponies and parties, of friends and servants, of ancestral portraits and silverware that represented not just wealth but a life outlined for her by an unbroken line of connection going back eight or ten or more generations, who carried in her head still the greatest wealth of all in the form of an education that was as useless to her now as it was rare. *Beati pauperes spiritu; quoniam ipsorum est regnum caelorum.* She was poor indeed, in both body and spirit, but how would knowing it in Latin help her? How would it buy her food? How would it buy her shelter and clothes? How would it find her friends? How would it help her recreate a network of connections in this foreign land where even her pronunciation of their common language set her apart? How could she, who had inherited everything, even the ranching business she continued when Ian died, how could she now at seventy-two build a life out of nothing in a land where she had not even citizenship? How? Everything she now owned—a change of clothes, the wedding ring she no longer dared wear, her canceled credit card and Argentinean driver's license, less than twenty American dollars—she carried in her pack, a homeless turtle with a faint, mocking adumbration of home on her back. What would she do to survive?

That thought brought her situation into focus. It wasn't a question of recreating or reclaiming what had been lost; it wasn't even a question of earning a living or creating a new life. It came down to something much more fundamental, the whole thread of her existence reduced to the immediacy of an animal's thread of DNA. There was no longer yesterday or tomorrow, regret for the past or dreams for the future. There was only the animal's immediate urge, to eat, to sleep, to pee, to stay alive, each need taken as it came. There was only now, this particular moment and need, to be forgotten as soon as the next one came, the next one not to be thought of until it arrived with its unknown yet imperious demands.

The panic and grief she had felt almost continuously since she fled out the kitchen door of *El Rincón* were gone, inadequate responses to the enormity of her situation, and in their stead came something almost like calm, an acceptance akin to lying on the hospital gurney prior to surgery— "We're going to start the anesthetic now, Mrs. Trevelyan. Please count backward from ten."—her life in other hands, other wills, no longer responsible for any action other than her measured breathing of polluted air in this foreign city.

A bit. As a child she had once put a horse's bit into her mouth to see what it might be like for the horse and what she retained was the foreignness of that taste in her mouth, the absolute, saliva-inducing unnaturalness of the taste of metal. That was what the air smelled like in Hollywood, California.

Sometime during the middle of the day she became aware of Tony standing over her and realized she must have fallen asleep. He had a Styrofoam cup in one hand and a package of cookies in the other.

"I told you. He okay." He gestured with his head toward the station building. "We got an understanding, me and him."

The coffee was foul, lukewarm colored water, weak and bitter from far too long on a burner. She thought of the *café con leche* of home, and wondered how America had ever earned its reputation as a land of coffee drinkers. The cookies were dry and sickly sweet. She ate them all, using her tongue to get the last crumbs out of the cellophane. She sucked the last drop of sour liquid out of the cup. Whatever caffeine it might have originally contained had long since been burned away and she promptly fell asleep again.

She woke with her head against Tony's arm. He was still talking to himself, but silently now, his lips moving, and gesturing with his free hand, guarding her rest by day as he guarded her person by night. When he saw she was awake he got up and went back out to the sidewalk with his broom and resumed sweeping.

That evening they walked back up toward Griffith Park, zigzagging onto Fountain and Sunset and Hollywood, and once onto a street named Cahuenga, stopping at the restaurants that would give away leftover food. They walked into the alleys behind and sometimes Tony knocked on the kitchen doors and sometimes they just waited. Sometimes food was offered, and sometimes a head would appear, Hispanic or black, occasionally white, once an Asian, and say, "Nothing tonight, Tony," and his reply to food or refusal was always the same, "Thank you, boss," spoken without gratitude or recrimination, flat, toneless, devoid of any emotional hook anyone might hang a response on. By the time they got back into the park they had eaten cold egg rolls and cold cooked broccoli, some hot chicken cooked with curry, and a variety of breads. As survival, it wasn't bad. It simply was what it was, in the same way and much to the same degree that it was for the cattle grazing in the fields around *El Rincón*.

It was the issues of sleeping and bathing that were most troublesome. Her body always felt greasy and she could smell her own armpits and vaginal smell in a way that repulsed her, but none of the homeless who lived their hidden lives in the bushes of Griffith Park seemed to share her fastidiousness. Three of them, two black, one white, had tried a haphazard and only marginally successful degree of organizing the bushes and their denizens, digging a shallow latrine in a densely hidden area near the overpass wall, but many of the men and women who came and went either didn't realize it was there or didn't bother to use it, and she couldn't bring herself to pick her way through. The area smelled worse than she did.

"Tony, where can I clean up?"

He neither looked at her nor responded, but he stopped his unending conversation and she knew he was considering the question.

When they reached Franklin, he jerked his head. "Come on."

They turned toward the east walking through progressively more residential neighborhoods, past the never-ending flow of cars, past buses, occasional joggers, bicyclists, people walking dogs, a few mothers with children pushing prams and walkers, once a police car. The officer inside stared at them curiously: a giant black man and an elderly white woman, both clearly out of their element, but he didn't stop.

They came finally to another portion of the park, the beginnings of a golf course that seemed to blend into the mountains and up to the enormous, ridiculous, self-aggrandizing white sign. There was a small cinderblock building. Tony marched up to a door marked, "Women/Señoras," and that single word in Spanish made her feel safer than she had for a long time, but Tony stopped her.

"I watch the door. Anybody hiding in there, you yell. I come get them out."

There was no one inside. Nor was there any soap or hot water, but there were paper towels. She stripped down and cleaned herself as best she could. There were only a few of the paper towels left, so she was still damp when she put her clothes back on, but she felt cleaner, and she couldn't smell herself anymore.

The sun had just set when she finally came out, and the air was filled with a refracted golden haze that reminded her of Buenos Aires. She turned to admire the light on the mountain and the ridiculous sign, and froze, electrified. On the far side of the golf course, so far away she couldn't tell if it was a man or a woman, someone was cantering a horse, cantering to the east. For a moment the sound of the city, the voices of the children at a nearby playground, the diesel grumble of a delivery truck on the road below, a motor-cycle's shriek climbing in register, everything stopped, her world a vacuum chamber devoid of all sight and smell and sound, heart and breath held in check, only familiar golden light and a distant cantering horse. Then it was gone and she gasped in delight and longing.

"Tony! Where do they keep the horses? Where do the horses live?"

He didn't know. He saw them occasionally when he came to this part of the park, but he didn't come here often. He thought they lived over by the river somewhere.

The vanished past drove her, shaped her, formed the outline of her life. Not just her personal past, the memories of Risada and a hundred other horses stretching back to the stables behind the childhood home outside Paraná, but the distant past, the lives and actions and instincts of people long dead, a generation ago, ten generations ago, a thousand years ago. She had an image of stables and green pastures on the banks of the Río de la Plata estuary, the water stretching out brown and blue to Uruguay, to the Atlantic, an oasis of the known and familiar in this foreign city. She would go there. She would find the horses.

Part III

Los Angeles, 1983

THE LA EQUESTRIAN CENTER, like so much else in Los Angeles, is not quite what it appears. For one thing, it's not in Los Angeles. It's in Burbank, and it started life as the Hollywood Cricket Club, where David Niven, Boris Karloff, Errol Flynn, Cary Grant, Ronald Colman, Laurence Olivier, P. G. Wodehouse, and practically every other British ex-patriot played cricket, whether they wanted to or not, at C. Aubrey Smith's invitation. It was an invitation only in the technical sense of the word; if you were an Englishman, and capable of struggling up out of your wheelchair unassisted, you were expected to play. The original old pavilion still exists, but the fields have been replaced by a massive covered arena, a restaurant and club house and offices, multiple smaller outdoor arenas for jumping and dressage and arena polo, stables for boarders, stables held vacant for the many equestrian shows and events the center hosts, and of course parking lots. Its seventy-five acres teeter on the edge of the graffiti-covered concrete culvert that is technically considered to be the Los Angeles River, a filthy, brown, litter-choked trickle of water that swells somewhat during the rainy season, and once every ten years or so, when El

127

Niño hits, turns into an impressive and deadly torrent that fills the entire culvert, sweeping unfortunate dogs, foolish men, trees, debris, rocks, sewage, drugs, and poison out into the ocean.

Like most people, I am a creature of habit, and on early Sunday mornings, unless the place was jammed with a Grand Prix or cutting or rodeo or some other event, I always liked to park behind one of the small outdoor arenas and walk up to the stables where I kept my horse. I had a Chesapeake Bay retriever, Max, brown, curly-coated, yellow-eyed, amiable, who went everywhere with me, and the little walk gave him time to empty out before I locked him in a vacant stall to wait while I rode.

At the aisle of stalls I turned and called to my horse. He was standing at the door, his head out, and he turned now to look at us, Max and me, with that complete concentration of animals, prey animals in particular, eyes, ears, nose all focused on us, assessing risk, weighing the known against possible danger.

"Hello, my sweet boy. How's my darling this morning?"

I leaned forward and inhaled the horse's sweet breath.

Max was already nosing at the next stall where the door was closed top and bottom. All the stalls past my thoroughbred were vacant, and the doors were kept shut, but Max was used to being put in the nearest one while I rode, and he was sniffing now at the threshold. Dogs too are creatures of habit. I thumped his side and opened the door for him. We both stopped.

An elderly woman was sitting blinking in the shavings, holding a dirty canvas backpack, shavings stuck to the side of her face, shavings scattered through her hair as they might cling to a horse's mane or tail, feet bare, shoes beside her, a coat spread over her legs.

What did she think as she sat there squinting in the sudden light? Did she even see me, or did she see a stocky, broad shouldered man in another stall in another land? I try to see myself as she might have seen me then, but the image is confused with my own vision of myself as I look back, vain and self-absorbed, with the false confidence of someone who has never known real defeat or real desperation. However she might have perceived me is blunted too by my memory of her in that first moment in a horse stall—wary, proud, bold, autocratic. All that from an elderly woman with shavings in her hair.

What did I say? I don't remember. What did I think? I don't remember that either. Perhaps I thought she was changing her clothes. Perhaps. It's not likely I thought of her as a homeless person because the homeless I saw on the streets as I drove from places of comfort and privilege—the equestrian center; Universal Studios where I earned my living; Hancock Park, the elegant residential area where I lived and where Pamela spent her first destitute night—those homeless people were mad or alcoholic or drug addicted or all three, and this woman, even with her worn and dirty clothes and with shavings in her hair, had presence, a sense of self, pride.

I probably apologized for disturbing her, called Max out and put him elsewhere. It was an odd thing, an unexpected tilting of my routine, but nothing more, and in the rarified bell jar of my life back then, trying to juggle too many elements in too few hours, I gave her little further thought.

The next time I saw her was a week or so later at a practice game in one of the outdoor arenas. It was the horse I noticed first, a tall, white-stocking bay I recognized immediately as belonging to one of the other polo club members, a young man who kept his horses up the aisle from me and traveled a lot.

She was wearing the same slacks I had seen, the same practical walking shoes, and the only concessions to riding were the horse leg-wraps around her calves. Even that was not especially remarkable. Players grabbing a few quick chukkas sometimes didn't bother to change into riding pants and boots, so I gave it no thought. The only thing that did strike me was her playing; she was excellent, far better than I or any of the others.

Most of us who played arena polo back then were young enthusiasts who had only recently made enough money to take up the game, and we weren't very good. Some of us were lousy. And arena polo was for people with limited resources. The real money, even if they were newcomers to the game like Sylvester Stallone, kept strings of ponies in Santa Barbara or Palm Springs and played outdoors with their own teams, and looked down on those of us with only one or two horses kept in stalls that cost more per month than my first apartment on the Lower East Side of Manhattan. We were all nouveau riche, but some were riche-er than others. And all of us, regardless of athleticism, were limited in our skill by our unfamiliarity with polo.

Here was a woman who was at least forty years older than anyone else on a horse that day, but she dominated the game.

It was after that game that I asked someone who she was.

"She's working as a groom for Joe."

"I thought Joe had a groom. What happened to the little blonde who was working for him?"

"He caught her stealing some stuff."

That was that. I thought it odd a woman in her seventies should be working as a groom, but I was far too self-absorbed to give it much thought beyond that.

As weeks and months went by I became accustomed to seeing her, sometimes playing in place of the peripatetic Joe, sometimes simply carrying out her duties as a groom. Joe did something with investments, something illegal as it turned out years later, and was richer than the rest of us, so she had four horses to keep legged-up, bathed, groomed, tacked and wrapped for games, and to play on when he was out of town. A lot of the young grooms, all girls in love with horses, made a great show of busyness and hustle whenever there were games. The old lady didn't. She didn't need to. She made up with efficiency for what she lacked in speed, and the same was true when she played. She was always in the right place at the right time. What her hitting lacked in power it made up for with accuracy.

I learned her name was Pamela, and when I spoke to her occasionally, briefly, I learned she had an English accent, was well educated, and while she was perfectly polite, she was neither friendly nor forthcoming, as if British reserve were something bred into her.

More weeks and months went by, and one evening Max and I drove out of the Equestrian Center and turned onto Riverside Drive and as I passed the first bus stop I saw Pamela sitting, waiting.

Aldous Huxley—or perhaps Alexander Wolcott or Dorothy Parker—once described Los Angeles as, "seven suburbs in search of a city." Regardless who said it, it was true then and truer now, and the city deserves credit for having any kind of bus system at all, even one that moves with the speed and efficiency of tectonic plates. You can get anywhere by bus as long as time is meaningless to you. I pulled over and walked back to her.

"Hi, Pamela. I'm Jameson. I keep my horse just down the aisle from you."

"Yes."

"Are you waiting for a bus?"

"Yes."

"Well, if you're going anywhere in my direction, I'd be more than happy to give you a lift. Where are you headed?"

"Hollywood."

"Hell, I go right through there. Hop in."

So it began. I got into the habit of driving her back in the evenings to the corner of Vine and Santa Monica, always to that corner, where there was a Shell station that seemed to hold some significance for her. She had a room just off Santa Monica and somewhere east of Vine, but she wouldn't let me drive her there, preferring always to walk. Sometimes I would see her at the bus stop and pick her up, sometimes I would wait for her at the stables, and sometimes she would tell me to go on, that she had too much to do, I would have to wait too long. When she did tell me to go on, there was no false longing, no coy oh-I-don't-want-to-put-you-to-any-trouble, any more than there was great effusiveness in her thank-you's. Everything was polite, matter-of-fact, and spoken with complete authority, spoken in a way that precluded any arguing with her. If she wished to be driven, I would take her; if she didn't, I would go on.

We never learn about people straight out, all at once, or even in a logical sequence of events, and in Pamela's case it was even more sporadic. She was not, as I said, forthcoming. She was polite in the detached and formal way we associate with the Queen, but it was always my question and her response. She clearly hadn't a clue what I did for a living, that *Simon & Simon* was one of the highest-rated shows on television, or even that a show called *Simon & Simon* existed, and as I was always slightly uncomfortable with my own success, and she was formally, politely, reticent about herself, I was content to keep the conversation in the neutral harbors of horses and polo. But I do remember how her story finally began to come out, piecemeal, in small chunks, and in response to my curiosity. It began with something she said about polo in Argentina.

"Oh, have you played polo in Argentina?

"That's where I'm from. I'm Argentinean."

"But your English is… I mean, I thought you were English."

"My parents were from Great Britain and maintained their British citizenship, but I was born in Argentina and I have only ever been an Argentinean citizen."

There was something about the way she said it, something resonating beneath the surface, that I could neither identify nor even precisely put my finger on. If I had to categorize it, I would say now it was defiance.

What did I know then of Argentina? What does any American know about how most of the world lives? We live in Camelot, safe and secure within the walls of democracy, a constitution, an impartial system of laws and justice, wealth, power, influence, military might, a sense of Divine ordination and superiority. We know nothing of the anxiety much of the world goes to bed with every night, the uncertainty with which they rise in the morning. Today, thanks to both television and the internet, the abuses and brutality that are common throughout most of the world, from Syria to Sudan, from North Korea to Somalia, from east and west and north and south around the globe, are becoming better known. But back then, if you had asked me to associate something, anything, with Argentina, I would have said, "Don't cry for me."

Gradually, over weeks and months and in erratic leaps and spurts, her story came out.

I don't know if it was the last time I saw her, but it is the last memory I have of her. It was an early summer evening like any other, light and heat and pollution lingering over the city as we drove down Vine. What were we talking of? I don't remember. Perhaps she was telling me some of what she had witnessed and endured, for we had gotten to that point, or perhaps we were talking of horses, but as we got near the Shell station I saw an enormous black man with dusty matted dreadlocks, in a filthy trench coat, sweeping the sidewalk on the Santa Monica side. His face was impassive, only his lips moving, but he was so clearly one of the mad products of Ronald Reagan's closing of mental health institutions that I was about to point him out. I was about to say, "There but for the grace of God go I." But before I could say anything, she saw him.

"It's Tony! It's Tony! The man who saved me. Oh, pull over, let me out, let me out."

The voice that came out of her was not Pamela's, not the elegant and aristocratically reserved voice of Pamela; it was a child's voice, full of joy and eagerness.

I was in the right lane and traffic was crawling, so it took only a moment to pull up by the curb. She already had the door partially open.

"Tony!"

He looked up, but the ambient noise had clearly confused him and he looked off down Santa Monica.

"Tony," she called again and this time, as she waved, he saw her.

If I hadn't seen it I wouldn't have believed it. Madness and menace and years fell away from him. He was still a giant unwashed black man with a push broom, but his face was as transformed as her voice, youthful, happy, kindly, gentle. He opened his arms and she ran to him.

Memory warps and dims over time. I know the reality is that she ran to him as what she was, a tired, arthritic, seventy-four year old woman, stiff and shaky and slow on legs that could no longer be trusted to carry her as she wished, as once they had. But what I see now as I look back is the free and easy lope of a beautiful young girl running to her lover.

He dropped his broom and swept her up, her feet dangling, and spun her around. And then, without warning, without speech, they began to dance, the arrogant, elegant, head-snapping, hip-swiveling, graceful steps of a tango, first to the west, then back to the east, and the crowded and graceless Santa Monica Boulevard became for an instant as transformed as her voice or the black man's face, car horns fading, people watching, pedestrians stopping, faces peering out of cars, mouths open in astonishment, a single girl's face lighting up as she smiled, but most just staring, staring at the unusual, the unknown, the beautiful.

I'm a dreadful dancer—just ask my wife. I have no more musicality in me than an alley cat, probably less. I almost never even listen to music, but I swear at that moment on the corner of Santa Monica and Vine, I heard the hard passionate rhythms of a Spanish guitar, a piano sliding in underneath, the echo of a violin, the pulse of a string bass, the swish of silk, the excited beating of hearts.

Looking for more great fiction?
Check out our other titles!

BEARMANORMEDIA.COM